CLAUS

by
Shawn Zachary

Published by FICTIONWRITERS
in association with
LULU Publications

Cover Design
by
FICTIONWRITERS

Acknowledgements

With sincere appreciation to
Patricia Ann Anderson
for her faithful belief in my fiction
writing endeavors.

Dedicated to:

Lola Myrtle Kocher
&
Bernard Edward Kocher

CLAUS

CHAPTER I

December 24, 1994:

Roaring jet engines dominated the atmosphere at Patuxent Naval Air Base's airfield. After several trainer-jets landed, the last of them taxied to its tarmac area. The pilot, Captain, Joseph Edward Anderson, raised the cockpit cover and disembarked his craft. He stopped briefly to speak with a noncom officer, dressed in work fatigues, and then proceeded through a hanger door and into the flight locker room.

"Hey, Joe. Come here a minute," another officer called from across the room.

Joe stopped long enough to put his flight jacket in his locker; then returned to greet his friend, Hal.

"How'd it go today?" Hal asked. His face expressed an exuberant smile as he donned his flight outfit.

"Another day, another dollar. What are you so happy about?"

Hal paused long enough to reach in his locker and retrieve a small box. He opened it, exposing a diamond engagement ring.

"You old son of a gun," Joe said, displaying a huge grin. "Never thought you'd get caught. What the hell is the rest of the female world going to do without your being on the loose?"

Hal grunted while pulling on a flight boot and laughed.
"Want you to be my best man."

"So. Who's the lucky lady, or not so lucky lady? Jan?"

"Yep. She's pregnant."

"Aw, shit."

"It's okay. Been thinking about getting married anyway. This way I get two for one."

"You idiot." Joe shoved him on the shoulder. "You're something else."

"Going to give the ring to her tonight. We're supposed to go to a Christmas Eve get-together at Cooley's place. Why don't you and Sarah come along?"

"Naw. You know I'm not a party kind'a guy. Spending it at home with the wife and kid."

* * *

Joe stood gazing at the neighborhood through his glass storm door. Bright lights adorned houses and trees up and down the street -- his home not being any different. Sarah busied herself with adding tinsel to an almost completed tree. Jay-Jay, short for Joe, Jr., sat on the couch eating cookies.

"Can you come here and help me get the angel on the top?"

Joe responded without hesitation -- his six-two frame much more suited for the task than his wife's shorter stature. Even then, he had to lean and reach over the lower branches as Sarah kept a firm hand on his military belt. They were both laughing.

"Forgot to tell you. Hal's getting married."

"You've got to be kidding me. To Jan?"

"Yep."

Mission accomplished, Joe moved to take a seat by his son on the couch. "Hey, Tiger. Those were supposed to be for Santa Claus. Can I have one?" he asked, whispering in his son's ear.

Jay-Jay giggled; giving his dad the one he had already bitten while reaching for another whole one for himself.

"So. When's the big day for Hal?"

"Don't know yet, but he asked me to be his best man."

"Why so sudden?"

"Jan's got one in the basket."

"Oh, no."

"He seems to be real happy about it." Joe rose and turned to pick up Jay-Jay. "Okay, little man. You've got a big day tomorrow. Not only is Santa coming tonight, but you've got another birthday party to attend. Tell your old man how old you're going to be?"

"Free." Jay-Jay held up three fingers.

"Three," his dad corrected, and smiled.

Joe held his son forward as Susan kissed Jay-Jay on the cheek. "You make sure he finishes that cookie before you put him in bed."

Jay-Jay's bedroom was decorated to the hilt with sports equipment and model jet planes. A picture of Joe and his Academy football team hung on the wall. A smaller picture of him in game attire, kneeling on one knee with a football in his hand, sat atop a chest.

"All right young man. That cookie's got to go."

Jay-Jay held it up and placed it between his dad's lips.

"Thank you," he said, his voice somewhat muffled from the morsel between his teeth. He placed Jay-Jay in the bed and drew the covers up to his chin, then kissed him on the forehead. "Now, no funny business. Santa won't come while you're awake."

"Okay, Daddy. I be good." Jay-Jay clenched his eyelids tightly shut.

Joe smiled and turned to leave the room, shutting off the lights as he left. "Night, son."

* * *

June 6, 2000:

"Now, boys and girls. Afternoon recess is over. It's time to settle down," the teacher, Mrs. Graham, said.

A slow hush began to engulf the room.

"I know you're all anxious to get into our show-and-tell period. Ann, why don't you be the first?"

Ann got up from her chair and moved to the front of the class. "This is a rose. My mommy grows them in her garden. They smell real good. I think they're really beautiful. Don't you? . . . Thank you, Mrs. Graham."

"And, thank you, Ann. That was a lovely presentation." Mrs. Graham scanned the students. Next, we have Darren Kovacs. Darren, are you ready?

"Yes, ma'am. I sure am." Darren got up carrying a shoe box to the front of the room. "Hi. I brought my pet to show you."

As Darren removed the lid, his pet white mouse leaped to the floor and began scurrying between the rows of desks. Several of the girls began screaming and standing on their seats.

Jay-Jay jumped to the rescue, quickly cornering the small creature.

The class calmed.

"Well, that was quite an experience," Mrs. Graham said, a bit winded. "Jay-Jay. Since you're the hero of the day, why don't you go next?"

Jay-Jay arose and stood at his desk. "I'm not a hero. My daddy is. He's a pilot in the Navy." Jay-Jay reached in his pocket and withdrew a pair of flying wings. "My daddy gave these to me. He's overseas right now. He's the hero." Jay-Jay sat down.

"Thank you, Jay-Jay. That was very compelling."

The 'Show and Tell' period continued for the remainder of the class day.

The school-bell rang, and the students stirred to leave.

"Before you go, children, I'd like to thank all of you for sharing your stories with me and for making what I think has been a very productive school year." Mrs. Graham moved from behind her desk. "Have a wonderful summer vacation and I hope to see you again next year for the third grade."

* * *

Heavy seas canceled an earlier planned mission. After the waters calmed, Joe sat in the briefing room of the aircraft carrier receiving final instructions.

"Take-off is zero-six-hundred. That will be all, gentlemen. God speed."

A buzz of excitement preceded the pilots scurrying to reach the flight deck. Hal, code name Googles, and Joe, code name Rudolph, gave each other high-fives as they left the room.

Joe immediately approached his plane, deafened by the roar of jet engines. Painted on the side of his craft, Rudolph the Red-Nosed Reindeer hovered over a row of Christmas tree balls, each representing a mission. Beneath them appeared his code name and the title: Flight Leader.

With Joe's squadron in the air, the planes soon reached formation. Among the squadron pilots were Shark, Googles, Raven, and Beaver. Their assignment: to run ground support against an ongoing insurgency.

Joe was at his best when flying. That is, second only to being a great dad and husband. He loved his work and was one of the best at it. His thoughts rambled as he gazed through the cockpit's windows at the billowing clouds beneath him. Jay-Jay was his pride and joy. Joe's only hope was he wouldn't have to miss another Christmas without being home with Jay-Jay.

Joe's wing-man, Shark, broke radio-silence.

Shark: "Shark to Flight Leader. Two bandits at four-o'clock. . . . What in the hell are they doin' here? . . . Probably some damn Iranians."

Rudolph: "Flight Leader to squadron. Follow my lead."

The jets broke formation and dove to confront their targets as the bombers began to drop their loads.

Conversation filled the airwaves.

Googles: "I got the one on the right."

Beaver: "Move over. I got him. Comin' through."

Raven: "Watch out Goog. You've got one coming around."

Shark: "I got him, Raven."

Shark's plane lined up on the missile chasing Googles.

Shark: "Break left, Goog. Drop low and break left, damn it."

The missile exploded in mid-air.

Shark: "Got him, Goog. Oh, yeah. Got the bastard."

Two more ground-fired missiles seemed to appear from nowhere. An almost immediate puff of smoke flowed from Googles's plane as liquid spewed from one of his wings.

Googles: "I'm hit. I'm hit," he yelled, as blood oozed from his right shoulder, arm and thigh.

Raven: "I'm after you, Goog. Hold on."

Rudolph: "Flight Leader to Raven. Get back and clean up the mess. I'm going down after Goog."

Googles had finally managed to level his plane at a low altitude. Joe brought his jet along side of the crippled craft.

Rudolph: "Hey, Goog. I'm here. Hold it together. Switch

over to the alternate band."

Joe changed radio frequencies.

Rudolph: "You there?"

Googles: "Yeah. . . . I'm here. But, I can't make it. I'm hit bad."

Rudolph: "Come on, man. You can make it. I'll help you back to the coop."

Googles: "Won't work. Losin' too much fuel."

Rudolph: "Can you bail out?"

Googles: "Got a can opener?" Googles' left hand struggled to steady the stick. His right arm and hand lay limp in his lap. "Canopy's jammed. I gotta go down." Rudolph: "There's a flat area on the other side of those hills ahead of us. Keep your altitude. I'll go down with you and give you cover until a chopper can get in. Stay on this channel. I'm calling for assistance."

Joe switched his radio knob to a rescue channel.

Rudolph: "U.S. Naval Flight Leader to U.S. Ground Air Command. Mayday, . . . Mayday. I've got a wounded duck on the deck at Code Cherry Haven. Mayday, . . . Mayday."

The radio crackled in response.

Rudolph: "Mayday. Mayday."

A voice broke through the static. "Air Command to Flight Leader. Loud and clear. Have you on the screen. Get right on it. Over and out."

Rudolph: "Roger that. I'll maintain cover as long as I can. Over and out."

Joe switched back to the alternate band.

Rudolph: "Hey, Goog. Help's on the way."

No sooner had he completed his statement and a blinding explosion occurred leaving Googles's plane in pieces. Joe's jet was ablaze.

CHAPTER II

Sixteen Months Later -- Early December, 2003:

"Okay, class. Don't forget you have your essay to complete by Friday. You're dismissed."

The previously quiet classroom erupted into a buzz of conversation and bustle as students rushed to leave.

"Jay-Jay, could I see you for just a moment?" the teacher called out over the din.

Jay-Jay placed his books on his desk and approached the front of the room. "Yes, ma'am."

"I wanted to ask you something," she said. "The teaching staff of the seventh and eighth grades is working together to put on an exhibition of hobbies and crafts created by the students. Would you like to participate?"

"Uh, . . . I don't know," Jay-Jay said rather timidly.

"I understand you're quite a model-maker. Some of the students have told me about your model airplane collection. I hear it's really good." She smiled.

Jay-Jay perked a little bit. "Yes, ma'am. I like to make airplanes. My dad used to help me do them before his plane got shot down."

The teacher's smile quickly faded. "I'm really sorry about your dad, Jay-Jay. I've heard stories circulating about it."

Jay-Jay's eyes began to tear as he struggled to regain composure. "He's coming back. I know he's not dead. . . . He'll be back, I know it."

The young lad's pain almost caused his teacher to cry.

"I'm sorry, Mrs. Johnson. I just miss him so much."

Jay-Jay's teacher couldn't restrain herself any longer. She stepped forward and wrapped her arms around him as they silently wept together.

* * *

"Hey, Jay-Jay. Wait up," Skip called as they were both about to leave the school building. "Wanna play some basketball after we get home?"

"Sure. Sounds good to me."

"Okay. I'll see ya at the court in about an hour."

"Cool, dude."

Skip took off in a dead run as a group of girls stood off to the side. "Hi, Jay-Jay," one of them said as he passed.

"Hi," he replied, with a slight wave of his hand, and continued down the front steps.

Jay-Jay strolled across the school lawn as he headed for home. The day turned out sunny and fairly warm for an early December day.

"Jay-Jay. Wait up you loser," he heard from behind.

"Where ya goin, 'commie?'" another voice called out.

Jay-Jay looked over his shoulder, stopped and turned. A group of four schoolmates were following him. "Leave me alone, Jack." He started to walk away when he was grabbed by the arm. "Let go of me, George."

"What are you, chickenshit just like your old man? He wasn't no hero. He's one of them 'commie' defectors like the TV says."

"You son of a bitch," Jay-Jay said, almost in a scream of denial. He swung at George and missed.

A melee ensued with Jay-Jay getting the worst of it -- all four jumped him. They left laughing and jeering as he struggled to get up from the ground.

* * *

Before going inside, Jay-Jay stopped to brush off some remaining dirt on his jeans and get a drink of water from the garden hose. He knew his mother would still be at work, and glad of that fact. It would give him time to clean up and avoid a bunch of fuss, and he headed straight for the bathroom.

He stood in front of the sink and mirror tending to his abrasions and bleeding nose while struggling to hold back tears. Why am I crying, he thought. Because I'm mad. Yeah, because I'm mad at those idiots who did this to me. For what? My dad was a hero, not a commie-defector. They're wrong. He would never do that. He couldn't do that.

Jay-Jay wet the towel again with cold water and held it to his forehead as he entered his bedroom.

Both of his dad's Academy football pictures now sat on the top of his dresser along with a model of his aircraft and a War Department letter, listing him as a MIA. A thick candle sat beside the items. Taking a match, he lit it and stared into the flickering flames.

"Jay-Jay, I'm home," he heard his mother call from downstairs. "Can you come help me?"

"Yeah, Mom. I'll be right there."

Jay-Jay blew out the candle and stopped in the bathroom long enough to appraise the damage done to his face before going downstairs. He sounded like a herd of elephants thumping down the steps.

"Jay-Jay, how many times have I told you not to do that," his mother called from the kitchen.

"Sorry, Mom," he called back.

"There are more groceries in the car. Would you get them for me?"

"Sure."

While Jay-Jay busied himself with the bags in the trunk of the car, his next-door buddy Tony showed up bouncing a basketball. "Need some help?"

"Naw. No problem. Where ya headed?"

"Where else?" He continued dribbling the ball. "Skip said you were going to play, too."

"Yep. I'll be there after I get things done here. See ya in a little while."

"Okay, dude." Tony started to walk away. "What happened

to your face? You look like crap."

"Nothin'. I ran into a lawn mower."

They both laughed.

"All right, see you in a little while," Tony said, taking off in a run with the basketball cradled under one arm.

Jay-Jay's mom was busy putting away canned goods as he brought in the last bags of groceries.

"Oh, there you are. How was your day?" she asked without looking up.

"All right."

"That rough, huh?"

"I can't wait 'til school's out," he said, grabbing an apple and taking a bite.

"Wow. That is bad. You're not even halfway through the school year and complaining already." She laughed. "Anyway, I wanted to let you know my boss, Mr. Maxwell, is coming for dinner this evening."

"Why? What for?" Jay-Jay's voice indicated both concern and a tinge of disapproval.

"He's a very nice man, . . . and he's really been good to us."

Jay-Jay took a seat at the table while Sarah continued her chores. She turned toward the refrigerator and for the first time noticed Jay-Jay's face. "My God. What in the world happened to you?"

"Uhhh, . . . football. Playing football."

Sarah smiled. "Just like your father, you are." She paused while placing a gallon of milk in the fridge. "You know he had an offer to become a professional after his service time if he had returned home."

"You've told me that story a hundred times already. And, he ain't dead."

Sarah appeared stunned by his reaction. "What brought that on? What's wrong with you?"

"Mom, they say he wasn't a hero. They say he might be one of those commie-defectors."

"What? Where did you hear that trash?"

"It's on the TV, Mom. Why don't they know what happened to him?"

Sarah moved to kneel in front of Jay-Jay, putting her arms around him. "Oh, honey, honey. You've got to accept what's happened. . . . I know it's hard, but you have to face reality at some time." She paused to wipe away a tear running down Jay-Jay's cheek. "I didn't want to tell you this, but a few months ago the Navy changed the MIA status to having been killed in action."

Jay-Jay ripped away from his mother's grasp and jumped to his feet. "You lie. You're a liar. He's not dead. And, I don't want to see whoever's coming here tonight."

Out of reflexive reaction, Sarah reached out and slapped him across his cheek. "Don't you ever talk to me like that again," she said, almost in a scream.

Jay-Jay rushed from the kitchen as his mother cupped her hands over her mouth and burst into tears.

* * *

Night sounds and the distant shrill of a train's whistle filtered through the dark bedroom window. A faint beam of light from Jay-Jay's flashlight focused on various needed items.

A digital alarm clock indicated it to be near two-thirty, a.m., as Jay-Jay busied himself gathering clothes and other necessities into a duffle bag.

Before leaving the backdoor, he paused in the kitchen to quietly select several additional supplies.

* * *

Jay-Jay had walked across the bridge hundreds of times in his life, but never dared venturing to the tracks below. It was a childhood taboo to go near them. But, tonight was different. He stopped and looked over the bridge's rail, staring at the many train cars sitting in a row. He noticed activity at one train several hundred yards ahead.

He quickly left the bridge and headed for a chain-length fence built to ward off intruders to the yards. Tossing his sleeping and duffle-bags across, he immediately scaled the barrier.

He stopped long enough to survey the situation and couldn't see any boxcar doors open. Finally deciding a 'flatbed' was his only option, he ran across the divide, duffle-bag in tow, then climbed aboard.

No sooner had he reached his destination, than the train began to move. It slowly picked up speed, traveling through areas bordered by thick trees, interrupted with occasional breaks of road-crossings and industrial and residential sites. The train's wheels against the tracks reverberated a clacking sound against the rail splits.

Atop the flatbed, there were several skids of lumber with a small space between them. Jay-Jay decided it best to huddle in one of the open areas in order to brace himself from the wind.

After opening his sleeping bag and retrieving a blanket, he cuddled inside and soon fell asleep.

* * *

A jolt of the train uncoupling cars awakened Jay-Jay. He peered out of his sleeping bag and around the stacks of lumber while rubbing his eyes.

The freight train came to a stop on an outer track. Gathering his goods, Jay-Jay slipped from the train and headed toward a nearby barrier, following it until he reached an opening.

On the other side, and after climbing a steep incline covered with brush, he arrived at a street aligned with row houses.

A bit disoriented, he decided to go in the direction of the early mid-day sun. He had no idea what time it was, but figured it to be nearing noon. After walking several city blocks, he came upon an all-night diner. He stopped long enough to inspect a newspaper dispenser out front, and learned he was in Philadelphia -- not in the direction he'd hoped to go. Somewhat discouraged, but not totally dismayed, his stomach growled, reminding him he was hungry.

Jay-Jay entered the eatery and found a spattering of customers sitting at the long counter, and a few seated at booths along the front window area. He went to the far end and selected a stool away from the others.

A large man in a white shirt, cap and apron approached. "What'll it be, son?"

"Could I have an egg sandwich and some milk?"

"Breakfast's over. Want a burger, instead?"

"Uhhhh. . . . Yeah. Please."

The large man turned and leaned toward an opening in the wall and said in a loud voice, "An all-beefer and jerk on the cow."

Jay-Jay looked puzzled, then smiled.

While awaiting his order, he gazed around the room, deciding those present to be either homeless or certainly poor. His attire, although nothing more than jeans and a new warm jacket, was in great contrast to the clothes most of the customers wore. He suddenly found himself feeling sorry for them. He really didn't know why, but his mind rambled on in remembering the times he, his dad, and his mom had volunteered to work with others to provide Thanksgiving dinner to the unfortunate.

"You got money to pay for this?" the large man asked, breaking Jay-Jay's reverie, as he placed the sandwich and glass on the counter.

"Yes, sir," Jay-Jay said as he reached inside of his jacket into a shirt pocket containing a small wad of bills, exposing them just long enough for the counterman to see.

"That's good. But, you best be keepin' that out of sight. Least around here, if you know what I mean."

Jay-Jay nodded affirmatively and took a big bite out of his sandwich. He placed it back on his plate and reached for the ketchup and mustard.

* * *

After walking several blocks, Jay-Jay found himself in a small commercial district. He stopped occasionally, gazing through the windows at an array of various things on display. He eventually arrived at a small hobby shop where an array of plastic models sat on stands. As great as the temptation was for him to go inside, he fought the urge, knowing it best to ignore spending any of his funds on such trivial pursuits.

As he neared a street corner with a traffic light, an elderly lady spilled her groceries all over the sidewalk. Jay-Jay rushed to help her.

"You're a very nice young lad. Here. This is for your help." The lady pushed a dollar bill in his hand.

"Oh, no, lady. I can't take that."

"Oh, yes, you can," she persisted. It's for being so kind. And, I insist."

Jay-Jay smiled and thanked her, turned away shoving the bill

17

in his jacket pocket, and crossed the street to a small park.

While sitting on a bench, he befriended a small dog. Picking her up and placing her next to him, he retrieved a pack of vanilla wafers from his sack, sharing them, until he saw an approaching policeman in the distance.

He took off, posthaste.

CHAPTER III

Jay-Jay spent the rest of the day roaming the nearby streets, making sure not to wander too far from the rail yards. Night was fast approaching and, he reasoned, the best time to try to board another train.

He cursed himself for having waited until such a late hour to approach the yard area, and stood across the street contemplating his next move. He realized using his flashlight to show the way was not a good thing to do. Cautiously he proceeded through the wooded area toward the fence and the railroad yard. The full moon aided his sight as he moved quietly and slightly downhill along a path until seeing a flickering light ahead. The glow of a campfire became more apparent as he ventured further.

Jay-Jay arrived at a small clearing. He observed an elderly Afro-American man with graying temples wearing a skullcap and somewhat tattered clothes. The man hovered over the flickering flames.

Jay-Jay remained silent, standing at the edge of the woods, as the stranger tended to his cooking.

"If'n you gots a need to eat, come on over."

He was stunned, thinking he had surely been quiet enough not to have been heard. Jay-Jay didn't move. Several moments passed.

"Won't bite'cha boy. Gots some stew on my mind instead."

Jay-Jay moved forward very slowly, keeping the fire between them. "Smells good."

"Is good." The hobo smiled and chuckled. "Boy, if'n I wanted to, I could'a hid in dem woods and scared the wits outta you. Heard you comin' the minute you sat yous foot on that path. Put them bags down and have a seat. Nice to have some good company for a change."

Jay-Jay placed his gear on the ground and sat on his sleeping roll, crossing his legs. He didn't speak.

"Don't talk much, does ya?"

"No, sir."

"Now, I calls that nice. I ain't been called sir since I can't remember when." The hobo chuckled at his own remark. "What be's ya name?"

"Jay-Jay."

"Nice to meet ya, Jay-Jay. You kin calls me HoJo." He rose from the fire and set the large pot aside. "Well, the stew's done. Got a pot in that bag of yours?"

"No, sir."

"Lawd'a'mercy, boy. You's out here on the road and ya ain't got no pot. How's you plan on eatin'?"

Jay-Jay shrugged his shoulders and shook his head in an 'I don't no' manner.

Hojo reached into his belongings, retrieved another small pan, poured a large portion of his concoction into it, and handed it to Jay-Jay.

"Careful, now. Sip it easy. It be real hot."

Jay-Jay drew the pan near his nose and sniffed the aroma. "It sure smells like chicken. Something like chicken noodle soup. What is it?"

HoJo chuckled and dipped a spoon into his share, blowing on it before putting it to his lips. "No wonder it smells like chicken. It's chicken gizzard stew. . . . Found the chicken gizzards and some vegetables at the supermarket back there. They was throwed in the trash. You's be surprised at what ya can find in the trash behind a food store. . . . I added some potato and carrots. I come up with some onion too that done gave it extra flavor."

Jay-Jay had yet to take a bite, and sat holding the pan in front of himself. "What're chicken gizzards?"

"Take a taste and sees how ya like it. Sure won't poison ya. Good for the soul, and sure ain't fattenin'." HoJo again chuckled at his own humor.

Jay-Jay blew on the mixture and carefully sipped from the container. "Oooooo. That's great." He sipped again, and again.

HoJo's huge grin expressed his pleasure.

* * *

It was barely light when HoJo woke Jay-Jay. "Come on, boy. Ya gotta gets up if'n ya be's goin' with me.

Jay-Jay struggled to his feet and filled his bag.

"We's gotta hurry, now."

HoJo led the way to the railroad yard. Having found a hole in the fence, they stood on its edge surveying the area.

"Wow. There're so many tracks and different trains. How do you know which one to take?"

"Tells ya about that later. Now, that be's our train over there," he said, pointing away from the slowly rising sun. "Let's get a move on."

Jay-Jay followed HoJo in a dead run toward an open boxcar. As soon as they reached it, HoJo threw his bags inside and climbed aboard, as Jay-Jay followed.

"Phew. I be gettin' too old for this jumpin' 'round like a young'un." He laughed. "Jest settle down over in that corner and get some more sleep. It'll be pullin' out 'fore long."

Jay-Jay did as instructed, and was soon in dreamland once more. When the train first started to move, it disturbed him briefly, but only for a moment.

The long stretch of cars rumbled over the track gaining speed as it left the yard, passing through the outskirts of Philly.

A few hours later, Jay-Jay awoke to find HoJo sitting near the open door gazing at the mountains. He moved to sit next to his newfound friend. "Wow. That's something else. Never seen mountains like that before."

Hojo chuckled. "Dem's the Appalachians. Don't be scared, cause we be's comin' to a tunnel through one of them."

Suddenly, all went blacker than night. Jay-Jay froze in his

spot. As quickly as the dark had come, the boxcar was again filled with light.

"That was cool," Jay-Jay said, laughing for the first time.

HoJo chuckled.

"Where are we headed, HoJo?"

"Chicago."

"Wow. That's a big city. . . . Why we headed there?"

"Ya gots a lot to learn, son, if'n ya wants to become a 'bo.'" HoJo adjusted his position to confront Jay-Jay directly. "Chicago is likes one of dem hub-centers for all trains, likes Atlanta, St. Louis and a few more spots. They has trains headin' in all kinds'a directions. If'n you want to go west from Philly, you go to Chicago first."

"Cool. . . . But, how do you know which train to take?"

HoJo laughed. "It be's not that hard, boy. We hoboes can't walk up to some yard man and ask. We gots to use our heads to figure it out. If'n ya be's in Philly and want to go west, ya look at the markings on the side of boxcars to find out where's they's from. Whens ya find one marked from Chicago, or somewhere west of where's ya's at, ya know that be's the train ya wants."

"Cool. I would never have thought of that."

"We be's pullin' into Pittsburgh soon and gots to get off while theys unhook and probably add some cars. Ya best be's off'n the train whiles they does that. Too much chance a'gettin' caught."

HoJo knew what he was talking about. Shortly thereafter, their train came to a halt. All ready to go, they both threw their belongings to the ground and jumped from the train. They hurried from the center of the yard and stood on its edge atop a hill overlooking the area.

"Wow, it sure is big," Jay-Jay said. "Can I ask you a question?"

"Sure, boy."

"How do you know when a train is ready to leave?"

HoJo smiled and patted Jay-Jay on the shoulder. "Well, ya sees the train we just got off'n. Its engine is still a'runnin'. Dat means it'll be a'leavin' real soon . . . just as soons as they gets done changin' cars."

Jay-Jay was mesmerized with watching the exchange. The train did back and forth movements as cars were released and a yard locomotive would come in between and haul the designated ones off to a side track. The same procedure was used to add new cars.

"Yous can bet that train will be a'leavin' pretty soon. Figure ya's got another twenty, maybe thirty minutes 'fore she's on the move."

Jay-Jay had quickly become adjusted and feeling secure in HoJo's presence. "Do you really have to go south?"

"Yeah, boy, I does. Every year 'bout dis time I heads dat way. It's warm down dere and I gots some friends to see."

"Other hoboes?"

"Yep. We be seein' each other for a lotta years. . . . Best ya be's gettin' ready to get back on that train. I'll go down dere with ya."

HoJo and Jay-Jay slowly crept their way back between boxcars until arriving at their destination.

"That be your train over there. This be mine," HoJo said pointing in different directions. "I be headed for Memphis first, then ons to Atlanta, then Jacksonville." HoJo opened his bag, retrieved a small pot and gave it to Jay-Jay. "Here you goes. This should help a bit."

"I don't want to take your pan, HoJo. You'll be needing it."

"Hush, now, boy. If'n I didn't want ya's to have it, I wouldn't'a given it to ya."

"Thanks." Jay-Jay stuffed it into his duffle-bag.

"Nows, ya remember what I told ya. Ya just got to get your directions straight. Ya got 'em all messed up last time. Always makes sure which way the sun goes down at night. If'n yous gonna go west, go that way in the mornin'. But, the train may be pointin' in a different direction. And always look for the boxcar marks dat are further west than you are. If'n you make a mistake, get off'n the next stop and use the sun to help ya out."

"I'll remember, sir."

HoJo patted Jay-Jay's shoulder and smiled. "And, never stay on a car whiles it's sittin' in a yard. Get off and waits 'til it leaves agin. Try and waits 'til the last second to board her."

"Yes, sir."

HoJo grinned big again. "I still likes dat. Ya's a good boy, Jay-Jay."

"Can I ask a question?"

"Sure, boy. Sure?"

"How did you get the name HoJo."

HoJo laughed. "Ho comes from hobo . . . Jo comes from Joseph."

"Sure pleased to have met you, Mister HoJo. And, thanks for everything."

They shook hands.

HoJo grinned from ear-to-ear. "Don't forget. First chance yous get, ya buys another pot or two."

CHAPTER IV

Jay-Jay awoke in the middle of the night. It was a good deal colder than when he had fallen asleep. After getting out of his sleeping bag, he moved to the slightly open freight car door, huddling under his blanket.

The night sky was aglow in the distance, filled with stars he'd never seen before. The clatter of the train's wheels against the tracks began to alter to a slower pace. The passing scenery quickly changed from rural, to suburban, to that of an urban environment. The train slowed even more, eventually coming to a complete halt. He could see flickering flashlights headed in his direction.

"Aw, crap."

Jay-Jay gathered his things as fast as he could and exited the boxcar, scurrying beneath it, and heading in a direction closest to its edge. Finding himself in the middle of the huge yard, he ran helter-skelter across the many sets of tracks, and heard the barking of dogs behind him.

As he reached a brick wall, he ran along it's length until coming upon a ladder leading to its top. Jay-Jay climbed upwards and sprawled exhausted on the wall's ledge. He gasped to regain his breath and composure, while listening to the barking slowly fade in the distance away from him.

* * *

The sun shone brightly by the time Jay-Jay stirred. He awoke, raising to one elbow, finding himself at one end of a long viaduct, rubbing his eyes before noticing a small raccoon nuzzling his duffle-bag. He yawned. "Good morning. Where'd you come from?"

The raccoon eyed Jay-Jay suspiciously, then continued his sniffing.

Jay-Jay retrieved a crunched package of opened peanut butter crackers from his jacket pocket. He tossed one away from his duffle-bag. The raccoon immediately responded as Jay-Jay reached to unzip his sack.

He pulled out a tin of Vienna sausages and a small box of saltines. Opening the tin, and the crackers, he shared them with his new acquaintance.

"Don't be so greedy," he said. "I need some, too." He laughed. "You have any money? . . . If you do, I'll get some more."

The raccoon started licking the tips of Jay-Jay's fingers and the inside of the can until it was sparkling clean. Then, it crept underneath of Jay-Jay's blanket and snuggled up next to him.

"Oh. I see. Now that your belly's full, and you've been up all night, I guess you want to get some sleep." Jay-Jay laughed and shook his head.

The raccoon peeked its head from under the covers, looked at Jay-Jay, and returned to its seclusion after a brief moment.

Jay-Jay rose, stretched his arms and legs, and moved to observe his surrounding beyond the viaduct. A sudden burst of rain caused him to quickly return to his earlier retreat.

He decided he could catch a few more winks and crawled into his sleeping bag to get rid of the morning chill. The raccoon once more peered curiously at Jay-Jay, but accepted him covering them both with the blanket.

The drizzling rain stopped by the time Jay-Jay awoke about an hour later as an intermittent mournful whistle of a train could be heard in the distance. He stood and turned to see a large silhouette of a man walking toward him from the far end of the viaduct. He carried a huge sack over one shoulder and a strapped duffle-bag over the other, clutching a walking stick in his free hand.

Jay-Jay remained still, totally dumbfounded. As the stranger neared, he appeared to be of late age and an absolute double for Santa Claus, sporting a flowing white beard, with long white hair streaming from beneath a black skull cap. He was clad in an unbuttoned black peacoat, dungarees, and heavy work boots.

Jay-Jay's expression tippled between awe and fear.

"Good day, to you," the stranger stated in a deep and rich-toned voice. "Think there's enough room in this ravine for the both of us?"

Jay-Jay slightly nodded his head affirmatively.

The new arrival swung the bag from his shoulder, placing it and the duffle bag on the ground, and blew a sigh of relief. "Phew. . . . That's better now." He eased himself to sit on a large rock and removed one of his shoes, beginning to massage his foot. "Feels like I walked all the way from the North Pole, it does."

Jay-Jay remained silent and befuddled.

"Just a joke, it is. . . . My 'Bo-name' is Claus." He paused to remove the other shoe, repeating his earlier task of kneading his foot. "What might your name be?"

"Jay-Jay," he mumbled, avoiding Claus's gaze.

"Sorry. Couldn't hear you."

"Jay-Jay," he repeated, this time much louder.

The raccoon stirred beneath the covers and scurried from under them.

"Well, if that don't beat all," Claus said, with a huge smile. "Who's your little friend, there?"

"Don't know. Just showed up this morning," Jay-Jay responded, with a shrug of his shoulders.

The raccoon started sniffing Jay-Jay's duffle-bag.

"I think he's hungry, again. I know I am."

"What's on your menu for dinner?" Claus asked.

Jay-Jay pulled his bag to him and opened it, retrieving two cans. "Either baked beans, or Spaghetti'Os. . . . Got some crackers, too."

"Planning on eating them cold?"

"Guess I'll have to. I didn't think to get some wood before it started raining. But, I got my own pot."

Claus smiled widely, and reached for his own bag. "Let's see what we can do about that." He opened his sack and fumbled inside of it. "How does your beans and some corn-beef hash sound?"

"Pretty darn good."

Claus sat up a Sterno stove and brandished a skillet as Jay-Jay opened the tins.

* * *

The doorbell sounded a long and persistent ring.

Sarah walked slowly across the living room, carrying a handful of Kleenex, with her eyes swollen from crying. She opened the door.

"Mrs. Anderson?"

"Yes."

"I'm Detective Sanders and this is my associate, Detective Jeffries. May we come in?"

"Of course. Please forgive me. It's just that . . ." She burst into tears.

The officers paused for a moment as Sarah stepped aside, and entered the home.

"Please excuse me," Sarah managed to say between her sobs. She took a seat in a wooden rocker as the two detectives moved to sit on the couch across from her.

"We certainly understand your grief, Mrs. Anderson, and intend to do our best to get to the bottom of this." Detective Sanders reached inside of his coat and removed a note pad. "You mentioned your son was unusually upset the evening before you found him missing?"

"Yes. I think he had been in a fight earlier that day at school." Sarah paused to dry her tears. "Something to do with his father having been killed in the war."

"I don't understand," Detective Jeffries said.

Sarah again wiped her eyes and dabbed at her nose. "My husband was a naval pilot and shot down on a mission almost two years ago. For a good while he was listed as an MIA, and last August altered to officially having been killed in action. . . . Jay-Jay, my son, just found out and couldn't accept the fact."

"You mentioned a fight," Detective Sanders said.

"Could I get you coffee, or something to drink?"

"No thank you."

"Do you mind if I get some water?"

"Not at all."

Sarah left the room and returned shortly thereafter carrying a tall tumbler. She retook her seat in the rocker. "Oh, yes. The fight." She sipped from the glass. "He had a scrape and a bruise on his face. He said it was from football. But, something he said got me to thinking." She paused to drink again. "He mentioned the news media's recent attention regarding military defectors back during the Vietnam war. I think maybe he was teased or taunted about it and they fought."

"I see." Detective Sanders continued to scribble on his pad. "Kids can be cruel."

"There's something more. I had my boss home for dinner." Sarah dabbed at her mouth with her tissue. "Jay-Jay got really upset and became very belligerent. . . . I've never done it before, but out of harsh reaction, I slapped him across his face."

"Detective Jeffries appeared to be digesting the facts, acknowledging them with a slight nod of his head. "It doesn't make it any less important, but I seriously don't feel there has been any foul play." He picked up a photo of Jay-Jay from an end table next to him. "From what you've told us, it's more than likely your boy is taking his emotions out against you. May we use this picture of your son?"

Sarah nodded her head affirmatively.

"I think that just about covers it for now. We'll see that this photo is returned to you shortly."

The two detectives stood and crossed the room as Sarah rose and moved to the door.

"We'll do all that we can, but you must understand. These situations may take some time to resolve. We'll put out an APB on him right away over the wires. If you can think of anything else, please give us a call."

Sarah reluctantly shook her head in acknowledgment.

* * *

They were just finishing their meal as the raccoon tried its best to get into Jay-Jay's pot for an extra share.

Jay-Jay placed it on the ground and the small furry friend eagerly attacked it.

"Which way you headed," Claus asked.

"West."

"Any particular reason?"

"Never been there. I'm tired of the cold weather at home." Jay-Jay paused for a moment to collect his thoughts. "Had a grandpa who lived in California. He died before I was born. I've seen pictures of him when he was young and in the Army, though."

Claus nodded in recognition and wiped his beard with a checkered dishtowel. "Got any parents?"

"My dad's dead, too. He was a pilot and got killed in the war." Jay-Jay started to tear, and then regained his composure. "He was a hero."

Claus retrieved a canteen of water from his things and poured some in his skillet. "Hand me your pot."

Jay-Jay complied.

"I've got a son. Don't know where he is, but he's a pilot, too."

Jay-Jay's eyes brightened.

"Appears we have a bit in common." Claus swished water in the pot to wash it clean. "I'm traveling west, too. Mind if we tag along together for a spell?"

"No. That'd be great. I'd like that a lot."

"Good. Maybe I can teach you a thing or two about being a good 'Bo.'"

Jay-Jay grinned and nodded approvingly.

"You've already learned one lesson this morning. First thing you do is make sure you get some dry wood."

"Yes, sir."

Claus pointed to the raccoon. "You plan on taking Danny, there, with you?"

"Danny? . . . You mean the raccoon?"

Claus smiled while wiping out the pans.

"How come, Danny?"

"Daniel Boone's coonskin cap, of course."

They both laughed.

CHAPTER V

As the train traveled rapidly in a south-southwesterly direction, the surrounding terrain proved flat and dominated by fields of wheat and other grain crops.

Jay-Jay, Danny, and Claus rested at one end of the boxcar as two other hoboes occupied the opposite end.

A pronounced clatter of the trains wheels against the rails echoed through the car as Claus continued writing in a notebook.

"Claus," Jay-Jay said in a whisper. "Those two don't look right."

"Pay them no mind. You'll see their types every now and then before it's over with." He returned to his notes.

The two strangers continued having an inaudible conversation, frequently gazing in Jay-Jay's and Claus's direction. The smaller of the two rose and approached them. He carried a butt of an old stogie cigar stuck between his teeth. "Couldn't find a match. Thought you might spare one," he said.

Claus didn't acknowledge the man, or his request, and continued writing his notes.

Jay-Jay simply stared at the stranger.

"Hey. Just tryin' to be friendly. No need to be rude. . . . Got a match?"

Claus looked up in a brief glance with a negative shake of his head.

Without warning, the hobo made a quick grab at Jay-Jay's bag. Danny leaped forward hissing and bit the intruder's hand. The man screamed in pain and fell backward to the floor as his larger counterpart rushed to his assistance and made a similar attempt at stealing Jay-Jay's goods.

In a lightning like fashion, Claus swung his walking stick with great authority, hitting the second hobo across the side of his knee. The larger hobo crumpled to the floor moaning and gasping in pain.

Jay-Jay restrained Danny, as his small pet remained hunched and poised to strike again.

"Best be leaving us alone. Our little furry friend seems to be partial to Bo meat."

The smaller hobo's hand continued bleeding as he assisted his groaning friend back to their corner where they cowered and attended to their wounds.

"Wow. You were cool. I was scared as hell."

Claus had quietly resumed his writing and didn't look up, but smiled. "Just another lesson learned, but no need for profanity."

"Yes, sir."

The train continued to race through the flat-land area of rural farms and small towns.

* * *

The Maryland police station teemed with activity. Phones constantly rang with people coming and going, as others sat at various desks filling out reports and taking statements.

Detective Jeffries sat at his desk talking on the phone. He had no sooner ended his conversation, and the instrument buzzed again. He responded to the call.

"There's a Sarah Anderson on line-three."

"Thanks. I'll take it." He punched a button. "Yes, Mrs. Anderson. How can I help you?"

"Detective Sanders?"

"No. This is Detective Jeffries. Sanders is out on call. May I help you."

* * *

Sarah sat at her desk looking forlorn with the phone cradled to her neck and against one ear, fiddling with a stack of papers. "This is Mrs. Anderson. I'm calling about my son, Jay-Jay."

"Yes, Mrs. Anderson. We've had no word as yet, but I want to assure you we're doing everything we can at this time."

"Damn it," she said, sobbing. "It's my boy . . . my son." She paused to wipe her eyes. " Please. . . . Help me."

"Mrs. Anderson, I've got a boy about your son's age. I can really relate to how you must feel. Kids can be pretty headstrong sometimes and, from a lot of experience, when someone doesn't want to be found, they can do a lot to avoid it." He paused for a brief moment. "Believe me. We're not taking this lightly. We're doing all we can right now."

* * *

Jay-Jay noticed the train beginning to slow. "Where are we at?"

"We're coming into Kansas City."

"Why do people do that?"

"Do what?"

"What they just tried to do."

Claus placed his notebook beside him and adjusted his position. "It's the nature of the beast. The curse of mankind. Always wanting what one doesn't or can't have."

"But, we had a match. Why didn't you give him one?"

Claus smiled and then began to chuckle. "When you've been around as long as I have, you learn a lot about people and their true intentions. It wasn't a match he wanted. He was testing to see how far we would go to protect what was ours."

Jay-Jay gazed at Claus with a puzzled expression.

"Think about what happened. Danny sensed the wrong and danger before you did. That, not so dumb, animal's instincts knew of evil intent and protected both you and I."

Jay-Jay smiled and hugged his furry friend.

* * *

The train slowed to a snails pace.

Claus stood near the door peering at the station's surroundings. "It's a bad time to arrive at the yard. Get ready to leave as fast as we can."

They both gathered their things.

At the boxcar door, Claus hesitated and dipped into his bag, retrieving some ointment, gauze and an Ace-bandage, tossing them to the two hoboes. "Merry Christmas, ahead of time. . . . Ho, ho. Ho, ho."

* * *

Jay-Jay and Claus strolled down a shop-laden street carrying their belongings -- Danny getting a free ride with his head poked out of Jay-Jay's duffle-bag.

"Where are we going?" Jay-Jay asked.

"Got some things to get done. . . . There's a park up the way. You can wait there with Danny until I finish my chores."

Jay-Jay followed Claus's instructions as his Bo friend entered a Post Office across the street form the small park which was filled with noontime activity -- people going to lunch, or simply taking a stroll -- the weather being unusually tepid.

* * *

Claus patiently waited in line at the service counter to purchase a postcard, before moving to a side counter to complete his task, then deposited his brief note into the 'out-of-town' mail slot.

* * *

Jay-Jay watched as Claus exited the Post Office and walked to a drugstore and a pawnshop a few doors away. He turned his attention back to Danny, softly stroking his coat.

"That's an odd breed of dog you've got there."

Jay-Jay reacted as if stunned by a bee-sting, turning to see a local city cop hovering over him.

"Are you from around here?"

"I, . . . uh . . ."

"How come you're not in school? Where do you live?"

"What's the problem, officer?" Claus asked, surprising the policeman almost as much as Jay-Jay had been.

The cop spun on his heels, confronting Claus face to face.

"My nephew was waiting for me while I went to the Post Office."

"I, . . . I . . . ," the man in blue stammered. "What's with the raccoon?"

"Why? Is there a law in Kansas City about having a raccoon

34

as a pet?"

The officer stared at Claus -- his expression slowly altering to a more mellow state. "No. . . . No. Not that I know of. I was just . . . ." He appeared to be totally embarrassed. "Have a nice day." He quickly walked away.

Claus turned to Jay-Jay. "Feel up to grocery shopping?"

* * *

The hour had become quite late. Jay-Jay and Claus carried their paraphernalia while approaching a warehouse and climbed through a gaping hole in a chain-length fence. They proceeded to the rear where Claus pushed aside loose boards covering a ground-level window, urging Jay-Jay to enter. Once inside the building, Claus lead the way to an upper-floor area.

As the two reached the second level, they entered a large room. At its far end, a small group of hoboes sat gathered together -- an old oil barrel holding a small fire placed between them.

"Lawd, a'mercy. If it ain't old Claus. I can't believe my eyes," Pops said as they approached.

"You old reprobate," Claus countered. "I figured you'd be in Florida, by now."

"I figured you'd be at the North Pole, too," Pops said, and heartily laughed.

They all joined in.

"Last we heard, you had up and died some time back, maybe fifteen or so years ago," Pops continued.

"Me?" Claus motioned to Jay-Jay to move to the warmth of the barrel. "Goes to show you how rumors can fly."

Jay-Jay followed Claus's lead and placed his belongings amongst the circle of friends near the fire, as Danny poked his head out of his duffle-bag.

"Oh, wow. What is that?" Buzzboy excitedly asked.

"A raccoon. My pet. His name is Danny," Jay-Jay responded.

"Oh, wow. Can I pet him?"

"Yeah. I guess so. But, go slow. Sometimes he doesn't take kindly to strangers."

Buzzboy slid across the floor and let the raccoon sniff his

35

hand for several moments before petting his head.

"Who's the young'un?" Pops asked.

"He's Jay-Jay. We met up back in Chicago." Claus took a seat after warming his hands. "Wants to be a Bo like the rest of us."

"Ain't no future in that," a drunken voice said in a slurred manner.

Claus glared in the direction where it originated, as the Bo stirred and raised to his elbow.

"Pay him no mind. That's Vino. He's harmless. Just got a taste for the stuff," Pops said. "By the way, sorry about my manners. The other two are Chili and Buzzboy." He pointed out his additional two companions and responded to them. "This old white-bearded grizzly is Claus."

Vino tried to get up and fell backwards as Chili nodded recognition. Buzzboy continued to be preoccupied with Danny.

"Pleazzzed to meet'cha, Santa Claus," Vino said, and then started singing. "All I wants for Christmassss is a big bottle of 'Jack. . . . A big bott . . ." He let out a large burp.

Buzzboy and Jay-Jay giggled.

Claus ignored Vino completely and addressed Jay-Jay. "You can do what you want, but if I was you, I'd be considering getting some sleep. We've got an early train-time in the morning."

Jay-Jay responded immediately and readied his bed on the other side of the fire away from the rest. Buzzboy settled next to him -- Danny in the middle. A low volume conversation continued between the two new friends.

"Is he really Santa Claus?" Buzzboy asked.

"I don't know. I don't think so," Jay-Jay answered, wondering why a grown man would be asking such a question. It was somewhat apparent to him that his new friend had a mental problem of some sort.

"He really looks like Santa Claus." Buzzboy paused for a moment. "Do you believe in Santa Claus"

Jay-Jay adjusted his covers. "Maybe. I'm not sure."

"I do. In the morning, I'm going to ask him to get me a raccoon just like yours for Christmas."

* * *

36

Daylight was barely evident when Claus woke Jay-Jay the following morn. Pop, Chili and Vino were already awake and packing their belongings. Buzzboy was still asleep on the floor.

Jay-Jay realized Danny was gone.

We're going to miss that train if we don't put a move on," Claus said.

"I can't find Danny, Claus. I can't leave him. Where could he be?"

"Are you two a'leavin' with us?" Pops asked.

"No. We've got to find Jay-Jay's pet." Claus paused. "Are you going to leave Buzzboy behind?"

"He's got kin here. Said he wanted to stop and see them," Pops responded.

"Oh. You best be going on ahead. If we miss our train, we'll hang around until the next one."

"Nice to see ya again, Claus. Sure thought you was gone and buried, though." He chuckled and moved to embrace his old friend with a huge hug. "Hey. How about bringing me a nice big juicy lobster for Christmas." He laughed and turned. "Okay, boys. Let's get outta here. Florida's a'waitin'."

Claus and Jay-Jay began their search for Danny, and were soon distracted by flashing red and blue lights against the windows of the warehouse. They went to investigate their source, cracking one of the near blackened windows to peer outside. The local police were apprehending their three departing hobo friends.

Danny suddenly appeared, covered with the remnants of debris on his coat from whatever he had gotten into.

"That 'coon' is either the smartest animal I've ever known, or one of our luckiest charms." Claus smiled, petted Danny, and then laughed loudly.

Jay-Jay picked up the raccoon and brushed his coat clean with his hand.

"Come on. There's another way out of here," Claus said.

They started to leave, but Jay-Jay stopped and returned to Buzzboy. He placed Danny next to him and opened a pack of peanut butter crackers taken from his pocket, giving them to the raccoon.

CHAPTER VI

The cloudy sky delayed the coming of dawn as Claus and Jay-Jay located the proper train and open boxcar. Their first order of business suggested fixing a morning meal.

"That was a very kind thing you did back at the warehouse." Claus handed a can of Spam to Jay-Jay for him to open. "I heard you and Buzzboy talking last night before you fell asleep."

"I guess he'll really think you're Santa Claus, now," Jay-Jay said with a huge smile.

They both started laughing.

Jay-Jay finished the last bite of his food and wiped his mouth on his sleeve.

"Here," Claus said. "That's what towels are for."

"Do you think he'll be okay?"

"Who? Danny or Buzzboy?"

"Both of them." Jay-Jay got up to walk to the slightly ajar freight car door.

"Buzzboy has had a lot more problems in his life than dodging the police." Claus rose and moved to join Jay-Jay. "Danny's in good hands. Believe me."

They both gazed out at the passing mid-western scenery.

Claus continued. "You never did say why you decided to be a Bo."

"I didn't. . . . I mean, not that I didn't . . . I mean I didn't mean to become a hobo."

"Oh."

Jay-Jay returned to gather the dirty pans and utensils. "I just wanted to get away from everything."

Claus smiled and joined Jay-Jay. "That's what makes most of us a Bo."

Jay-Jay looked puzzled.

"Haven't you learned anything since you left home? I know for a fact that you've had more new experiences than you ever dreamed of having." Claus poured water from his canteen. "Every one of these hoboes you've met has some kind of a problem causing them to become what they are. Your friend last night, Buzzboy, didn't have the ability to tell you he lost his senses from a head wound he received in Desert Storm." He handed a pot to Jay-Jay to dry. "He wasn't as young as you thought. Not old, by a long-shot, but not a teenage kid, either."

Jay-Jay sat, showing great interest. "How'd you know that?"

"It's not important. The fact is, you aren't aware of what's going on around you. You have to be more cognizant of happenings, and causes." Claus finished the last of the utensils and got up to throw the used water out of the door, then returned to his spot. "Anyway, we're getting away from the subject of this conversation. Why did you leave home."

"What about you? Why are you a hobo?"

"Now, that's clever. Answering a question with a question." Claus chuckled. "Don't mind if I tell you the truth, do you?"

"No." Jay squirmed in his position to feel more comfortable.

"Well, I just got tired after all those years of the elves going on strike; the nagging of Mrs. Claus, and Rudolph taking off whenever he got the urge, and . . . ."

Jay-Jay's eyes grew wide. "Rudolph. That was my dad's code name in the Navy."

"Well, I'll be a monkey's uncle. If that don't beat all. That's quite a coincidence."

Jay-Jay stirred from his prone position to sit at full attention. "What do you mean by a coincidence?"

"It's not important." Claus turned to lean against the side of the boxcar. "My favorite reindeer was Rudolph, and your

Rudolph was your dad. That's all."

"Are you trying to tell me you think you're really Santa Claus?"

"Maybe, yes. Maybe, no. Think what you want to believe." Claus paused for a moment to stretch his arms and legs. "At your age, I guess you've stopped believing in Santa Claus, and the spirit of Christmas."

Jay-Jay shuffled uneasily in his seated place. "There ain't no Santa Claus. And, there ain't no God."

"Whoa . . . whoa . . . whoa, now, son. God didn't shoot your dad's plane out of the sky."

Jay-Jay's eyes began tearing.

Claus moved to sit beside the lad and put his arms around him. "War's a terrible thing. I know. I've seen death, devastation, and the broken hearts of families too many times. I'm sure your dad was doing the thing he loved best . . . flying. I doubt he enjoyed the killing, and the war he was fighting. But, he was fighting for freedom and a hope for future peace."

Jay-Jay rubbed his eyes with his sleeve.

"You don't have to believe in Santa Claus, but whatever you do, don't be angry with God. I know he was with him in the plane, and I'm sure he's with him now."

* * *

The doorbell rang as Sarah stood at the sink washing the dishes. She dried her hands and answered the door.

"Good afternoon, Mrs. Anderson. Here's your mail," the postman said.

"Oh, hello Donald. Thank you."

"I don't mean to pry, but have you heard anything more about your son?"

"Uh, . . . no." She felt a twinge at the mention of Jay-Jay. "Uh, I'm sorry. I don't mean to be rude. I just don't seem to think straight half of the time, anymore. Do you have time for a cup of coffee?"

"I sure do, Mrs. Anderson. You look like you could use some company, too."

Donald entered and followed Sarah to the kitchen where he took a seat at the table.

Sarah immediately retrieved two mugs from a cabinet, filled them with the black steaming liquid, and joined Donald. "I guess you'll be glad when Christmas is over. Have the deliveries been heavy?"

"Yes. And I sure will. Just another twelve days to the big day, but we still have a carryover after that." Donald paused to add sugar to his coffee. "Things don't really get back to normal until after the New Year. But, at least we've had some pretty good weather."

"There I go again. Somewhere off in space. Would you like some cream?"

"Oh, no. Thank you." He paused to sip from his mug. "It's been over a week since the boy's been gone, hasn't it?"

"Nine days."

"And, the police haven't been able to do anything, yet?"

Sarah shook her head in disgust and accidentally spilled some of her coffee. She got up to get some paper towels. "The police? They've been here once to talk to me." She returned, took her seat and began wiping up the mess. "I call them every day and it's the same thing over and over. Have patience Mrs. Anderson. We don't think there's been any mishap, Mrs. Anderson. The evidence indicates your son is emotionally upset and ran away, Mrs. Anderson. We'll contact you as soon as we know anything at all, Mrs. Anderson." Her eyes began to tear. "They don't even know if he's still around this area, or not."

"I know it's got to be extra hard on you because of the time of the year. I wish there was something I could do."

Sarah smiled, reached for her mail, and began fumbling through it. "Thank you, Donald. That's really kind." She started to separate Christmas cards from the bills. "I guess the season did have something to do with Jay-Jay's mood. His dad had never missed being home at Christmas to be with us, until he was sent to the Mid-East." Sarah paused as she noticed a postcard and began reading it. She gasped, and covered her mouth with her free hand. "Oh, my God."

"What is it? What's wrong?" Donald eagerly asked.

"The postcard. . . . This postcard. It's about Jay-Jay."

"What does it say?"

Sarah read it aloud. "Dear Sarah. Jay-Jay's fine. He's shedding his emotions. Don't worry. He'll be home by Christmas."

"Is it signed?"

"No."

"Where was it postmarked?"

Sarah turned the card over. "It doesn't have one."

"That's odd." Donald chuckled. "I guess the Christmas rush was probably the cause it didn't get canceled."

"Yeah, you're probably right. . . . But, somebody wrote the card and mailed it. Who? Who's he with?"

"I don't know, but he must be okay. And whoever he's with must be a caring person, or why else would they make the effort to contact you. Whoever wrote that realizes you're worried and needed to know Jay-Jay's all right and in good hands."

* * *

"Where will be getting to next?" Jay-Jay asked, as he crawled into his sleeping bag.

"We should be arriving in Denver by near daybreak." Claus followed Jay-Jay's move and took an extra blanket from his bag and covered it over the lad. "You best be trying to get some sleep. We'll be up early in the morning. I'm going to write for a little while then catch a few winks myself."

"I will. Night."

Morning came a bit faster than Jay-Jay would have preferred. Claus woke him while it was still dark and, the temperature outside, bitter cold. "What time is it," he asked.

"Almost seven. We should be in the rail yard in about ten minutes. You best be getting your things together."

The train began to slow, proving Claus to be right.

Jay-Jay quickly gathered his belongings and the two moved to the door.

"We'll be changing trains today, so we best be sticking near the yard. It'll be about noon when our next one leaves."

"Yes, sir."

"And, when we stop, we want to clear out of here as fast as we can. The yard guards can be pretty tough around here." He chuckled.

43

Jay-Jay expressed a leery smile.

As the train came to a halt, they both jumped to the ground. No sooner than they did, a yard man carrying a bright flashlight could be seen several hundred yards away running toward them.

"Let's go," Claus said.

They both took off running as fast as they could across a number of adjacent rails, headed for the nearby woods. Once inside, the guard gave up on the chase and the two of them collapsed to the ground.

Claus laid on his back, almost hysterical with laughter. "I haven't ran like that in so long, I can't remember when the last time was."

Jay-Jay joined his jovial mood. "You didn't do so bad for being an old man," he said, laughing even harder.

"Watch out who your calling an old man," Claus said, while still chuckling. "That sure was fun."

Composure regained, they got up and moved further into the woods before stopping near the bottom of a steep incline.

"This looks like a good spot," Claus said, dropping his belongings to the ground. Why don't you get us some firewood, while I get us settled?"

"Yes, sir."

The day had just began to dawn and Jay-Jay shortly returned carrying an armful of sticks and short branches. Claus had already selected a few larger logs and immediately started a fire.

"There. That should help. You hungry?"

"You bet I am. Starved," he said, shivering.

"It'll warm up some soon. How does fried potatoes, Spam and eggs sound to you?" Claus asked as he brandished two cans, an onion, and a small carton in the air, taken from his sack.

"Wow. You can make eggs, too?"

Claus chuckled. "Sure can. Seems like you never heard of powdered eggs before."

"Nope."

"Well, they're not as good as the real thing, but not bad under the circumstances, either. Get me my skillet and pot from my duffle, and we'll get started."

The meal was more than Jay-Jay ever expected. His belly

was full and he felt truly relaxed for the first time in a long time. "That was really good, Mr. Claus."

Claus smiled. "Thanks for the respect, but Claus is enough. That is, unless you want to call me Santa." He laughed.

Jay-Jay smiled. "If you don't mind, I think I'll catch a few more winks until we have to leave."

"You go right ahead. I'll do a bit more of my writing."

"What are you writing about?"

"I'll tell you later, after I'm finished. Get some shuteye."

When Jay-Jay awoke, he found Claus putting out the fire.

"Well, now. That's what I call good timing. I was just about to get you up."

Jay-Jay yawned as he got to his feet.

"No need to rush. We still have about twenty-minutes before we have to board." Claus finished zipping his bag. "I've already checked things out and there aren't any freight cars open. We'll have to ride on a flatbed carrying a bunch of new cars piggyback."

When the proper time arrived, and taking great care not to be noticed, the two climbed onto the freight car.

"After we get out of the yard, we can sit inside of one of the automobiles to keep warm."

"Wow. That'll be neat."

The train slowly began to leave the yard as the two cowered close to the flatbeds floor so as not to be seen.

Once away from the station, Claus asked, "Feel like getting out of this breeze?" and smiled.

"Yes, sir. You bet I do."

"Well, let's climb up and pick a vehicle out. You want the red one, or the white, or the green? . . ."

"The first one we come to is fine with me."

Claus laughed.

"That's a pretty high climb, sir. Can you make it?"

"Just watch me."

They both started upwards, with Jay-Jay leading the way. He got to the first auto and tried to open the door, but it was locked. "Oh, wow, Claus. It won't open. They must all be locked."

"Let me check this out," Claus said, and Jay-Jay stepped

aside. As the lad turned away to watch his footing, Claus placed his finger on the lock and opened the door. "It must have been stuck."

"Oh, great," Jay-Jay said as he climbed inside.

Claus followed suit, sitting comfortably behind the steering wheel. As Jay-Jay peered through the window at the passing scenery, in awe at the mountains surrounding them, Claus touched the vehicles ignition and the engine roared to life.

Jay-Jay jumped as if shot. "How . . . how did you do that without a key?"

"We're just lucky, I guess. Whoever loaded this thing evidently forgot to turn the ignition off."

"Oh."

"How about some heat in here. Press that button beside your arm and lower your window just a bit"

Jay-Jay complied as Claus set the heaters temp controls.

"Boy, this is sure better than riding in a boxcar," Jay-Jay said with a huge smile.

Claus chuckled. "You bet it is, but most hoboes don't get this luxury." He pressed a button to make the seat tilt backward. "You can do the same thing to if you want to relax."

"Which button?"

"That one there."

Jay-Jay pressed the switch and his seat tilted as well. "That's cold."

Claus smiled. "Don't think I'll ever get used to you young'uns expressions."

Jay-Jay laughed. "Where are we headed for now?"

It'll take a while, but we'll be going to Provo, Utah from here. They'll make a brief stop there and drop off some cars that are designated for Salt Lake City. We'll be in the Provo yard in about an hour, but we won't have to leave the train. Just have to keep our heads down."

"How do you know all of that? The first Bo I ever met told me how to tell which way a train was headed, but how do you know that this won't be one of the cars dropped off at Provo?"

"Another lesson for you, son. I read the sticker on the back window and it says these cars are intended for a dealership in

Seattle. After we leave Provo, you'll get to see a real desert for the first time. Then, we'll be headed for Las Vegas. It'll be a couple of days or so before we get there."

CHAPTER VII

Claus opted to leave the freighter before it reached the main railroad yard -- the train having stopped a couple of miles short due to other rail traffic.

They walked down a highway toting their gear in the dark of the early morning hours, with the skyline of Vegas shining brightly before them.

"That's quite a sight, isn't it?"

"Yes, sir. It sure is. I never saw anything light up the sky like that except fireworks."

Claus laughed.

The sun shined brightly by the time they reached their destination. Following their long trek into town, Jay-Jay was dumbfounded when they arrived in the main gambling and tourist district. "This is unreal. . . . It's way too bad."

Claus smiled and shook his head. "How do you feel about having a great big fat hamburger?"

"That sounds so good, I think I could eat the whole cow."

Claus chuckled and steered Jay-Jay to a sidewalk café.

Two long rows of tables, placed under a canopy, occupied most of the space in front of the restaurant. The entrance doors sat open, exposing a lobby full of slot machines and numerous players.

Jay-Jay and Claus took a seat at one of the tables.

"I don't think I've got enough money left for this," Jay-Jay said.

"Never you mind. It's on me."

Shortly, a waiter arrived with a pad and pencil, appearing to be not especially happy having to serve his two patrons. "Do you know what you want?"

"We'll start with two cokes, and take a minute to look at the menu," Claus said.

The waiter made a note on his pad and walked away before quickly returning to bluntly ask, "You got enough money to pay for this?"

Claus reached into his pocket and pulled out a crumpled fifty-dollar bill. "Think that will cover our meal?"

The waiter sneered and retreated toward the kitchen.

"He was kind of rude, don't you think?" Jay-Jay said.

Claus took the two menus, handing one to Jay-Jay, and then began to browse. "Well. Think about it. If you had to wait on somebody dressed like us, carrying our homes on their backs, what would you do?"

Jay-Jay shrugged his shoulders.

"No. This is important," Claus stated. "What would you do?"

"If they were hungry, I'd probably get them what they wanted."

Claus paused as if engrossed in the menu. "Now, I'd call that a very charitable thing to do. But, if you did, and they couldn't pay, the owner would make you pay the bill, and probably take it out of your wages."

"Naw, he wouldn't. . . . Would he?"

Claus laughed loudly as the waiter returned with their drinks, placing them on the table. "Have you decided what you want?"

"As a matter of fact, we have. . . . We'll both have the same thing. A super-burger deluxe and two of those double hot fudge ice cream cakes for dessert."

The waiter again scribbled on his pad, took the menus, and started to leave.

"Uh, sir?" Jay-Jay said.

Their waiter spun around to confront them. "Yes. What is

it?"

Jay-Jay turned to Claus. "Do you mind if I have my fudge cake first?"

Claus laughed. "Bring him his dessert, waiter."

"I . . . I saw how big they were on the menu. I figured I could take whatever of the hamburger I couldn't finish with us."

The waiter stalked away.

"Would it be okay if I go look in at the lobby?" Jay-Jay asked.

"Sure. Why not?

Jay-Jay headed for the open doors and stepped in side. The room was filled with the sound of players pulling one-armed bandits and the tinkling of coins hitting metal. He slowly strolled through the rows of machines, most of them being occupied.

As he approached an elderly couple playing one of the slots, the lady pulled the arm and it was followed by a whir and the clicking of the windows images falling into place. Suddenly, coins began to tumble into the tray at the bottom. She had hit the Jackpot on a half-dollar machine.

"Oh, Herbie. We won. We won," she shouted.

Herbie bent over to gather several coins that had toppled to the carpeted floor. "Now, now, Alice. Calm down, honey. You know the doctor said you shouldn't get over excited."

Jay-Jay watched in amazement, then decided to return to his table. "Wow. I've never seen anything like that. It was too cool."

Claus smiled as their waiter arrived.

Jay-Jay delved into his fudge cake like a backhoe devouring dirt. Halfway through his sandwich he said, "Oh. . . . I can't eat anymore."

Claus was just finishing his dessert. "Have the waiter wrap it up like you said."

The waiter arrived with their check and Claus handed him the fifty-dollar bill. "Would you bring us a doggie-bag for the lad's sandwich." Claus pushed himself away from the table and brushed himself off. "You know. I think the waiter was right. We do look a bit scroungy. I could use a bath and a good night's sleep. How about you?"

"What do you mean?"

"Do you still have any of those silver dollars you said your grandfather left you?"

"Yeah. . . . Yes, sir. I've got two." Jay-Jay reached into his pants pocket and retrieved both coins.

"I only need one. You make sure you hold on to the other one and don't ever spend it. Keep it for good luck."

Claus stood as the waiter returned with their change. Jay-Jay did the same.

"Keep the change, young man. Merry Christmas."

The waiter appeared dumbfounded, and managed a sheepish grin.

They both gathered their gear and Claus lead the way into the lobby.

As they mingled among the people, Jay-Jay continued to be fascinated with the game play. He noticed that the same old couple had moved to a different slot. "This is too neat. Look at all the money in those machines."

"Come on," Claus said. "There's one open over there." He headed for a dollar-machine with Jay-Jay close behind.

"Are you going to play that machine?"

"You bet. Just one time."

"Can I put the dollar in the slot? Can I pull the arm down?"

Claus laughed. "It's against the law. You have to be twenty-one to play. . . . But, tell you what, though. Why don't you just blow on this silver dollar for luck."

Jay-Jay blew on the coin and crossed his fingers.

Claus inserted the coin, pulled the handle, and the wheels spun.

"Ain't it ever going to stop?"

Claus laughed as he touched the machine with his finger tip on each of the four windows.

The wheels began to slow and finally stopped exposing four 'lucky-sevens' in a row. Bells began to ring and a siren sounded.

Jay-Jay gasped. "Oh, my Go . . . gosh. I don't believe it. How'd you do that?"

Practically everybody in the place gathered around them, cheering and applauding, as two of the restaurant's officials arrived.

"Congratulations, sir. I'm the establishment's manager. You've just hit the fifty-thousand dollar 'Power Jackpot.'"

"Wha . . . what . . . how much did you say?" Jay-Jay excitedly asked.

The manager smiled.

"I don't believe it. . . . I don't believe it. . . . I can't believe it."

"If you'll follow me, I'll see that your winnings are secured."

The two shabby friends followed the manager to the rear of the room and into an office.

"Please have a seat," the manager said, as he pointed to two chairs facing him on the opposite side of his desk.

"I'm Harry Fine. And, you?"

"My name is Claus, and this young man is my nephew, Jay-Jay."

"Well, Mr. Claus. Our establishment is owned by the Casino Royal Hotel. We aren't prepared to transact that amount of payoff here. If you'll excuse me for a moment, I'll contact the hotel and have them prepare the necessary documents."

"Certainly. Go right ahead."

The manager fumbled through one of the desk drawers and produced a leather folder. "You do realize there are tax forms and other papers required."

"Naturally."

At that moment, a tall man in a chauffeur's uniform entered the room.

The manager pushed a button on his speaker-phone and a voice answered after a brief pause.

"Yes."

"Harry here. I have a Mr. Claus and his nephew with me who've just hit the 'Power Wheel' jackpot. I'm sending them over with George."

"I'll tell Lester," the speaker-phone responded.

Harry ended the call and opened the folder. He wrote on a form, signed it, and handed it to Claus with a second form. "This is a voucher stating your winnings. All I need is your signature on the receipt as having received it. And, George. Would you please take our guests luggage to the Limo? They'll be there shortly."

Claus inspected the voucher, signed the receipt, and handed it back to the manager.

"Thank you. George is waiting out front with the limousine. He'll drive you to the hotel."

The three stood at the same time.

"We thank you for your courtesy, Harry," Claus said, as he and Jay-Jay headed for the door.

"Uh, . . . Mr. Claus. Has anyone ever mentioned you look just like Santa Claus?" Harry said, and then laughed.

Claus didn't turn around, but over his shoulder replied, "Many times. . . . Many, many times." He chuckled.

Harry followed them to the curb as George opened the stretch-limo's rear door.

"Congratulations again, and take care," Harry said.

* * *

Jay-Jay had his face almost pressed against the darkened window, taking in everything he could see.

Claus sat across from him with his back to the front of the limo. "Have you ever rode in one of these?"

"I haven't even seen one before," Jay-Jay said, without altering his gaze at the vibrant neon passing scenery.

"You mean you didn't know they even have a TV?"

Jay-Jay turned quickly from the window. "You're kidding."

"No I'm not. Look here." Claus slid open the upper door of a cabinet built into a corner next to his seat, exposing a TV. He then opened a lower cabinet holding a small refrigerator and bar.

"Wow. They've even got sodas in there. Could I have one?"

"Sure can." He handed one to Jay-Jay. "Look to your left and open the console lid."

"Holy cow. . . . They've even got a phone."

"It's for talking to the driver and making calls anywhere you want to. It's called a cellular phone. You could even call your mother if you'd like."

Jay-Jay quickly closed the console lid.

"There's also a stereo and player in the panel above the arm rest beside your elbow."

Jay-Jay glanced at it, laid back against the seat, and stretched out his legs. "Wow, Claus. This is really something."

The limo arrived at the hotel, pulling into a large circular driveway under a huge canopy cover, and stopped at the main entrance.

A doorman opened the rear door as George exited the front.

The two weary vagabonds made their way to the tiled street waiting for their luggage to be retrieved. Jay-Jay started to pick up his duffle bag.

"Here. I'll take care of your things," George said.

Jay-Jay appeared reluctant to let his belongings go for a second time. Claus gave him a nod and a reassuring grin as they were approached by a man dressed in a white dinner jacket coming from the lobby.

"Right this way, gentlemen. Mr. Lester is expecting you."

The entry lobby was huge and luxurious, and Jay-Jay gaped with bewilderment. There were sofa and chair settings all over the place and the furniture of expensive design. Huge paintings adorned the walls as if it were almost a museum.

To the right side was an entrance to a restaurant and nightclub, and to the left a number of doorways side by side leading to what could be nothing other than a huge casino. One of the doors opened as another man appeared dressed in a black tuxedo. He walked toward them.

"Mr. Claus, how nice to meet you. I'm Frank Lester, the manager of the casino. Congratulations on your good fortune." He extended his hand to Claus and then turned to Jay-Jay offering another handshake.

"I'm Jay-Jay."

"Very pleased to meet you, Jay-Jay. If you and your uncle will follow me . . ."

Claus interrupted him. "Mr. Lester, I hope you don't mind, but Jay-Jay and I are a bit tuckered-out right now and would like to get a room. Can we take care of business a little later?"

"Of course. Absolutely. This way, please."

Lester lead them to the hotel registration desk, and addressed the desk clerk. "Avery. Would you call Webster for me?"

"Certainly." Avery pulled a phone receiver from beneath the counter and placed it to his ear.

Jay-Jay continued to be amazed with his surroundings and gazed in every direction.

"If you keep spinning like that, you're going to get dizzy and fall down."

Jay-Jay stopped. "This is the most beautiful place I ever saw."

"Thank you, Jay-Jay. I'm glad you like it here," Lester said, adding a smile.

Webster arrived through a door behind the long counter. "Yes, Frank. What can I do for you?"

"Webster. These two gentlemen are to be guests of the hotel for the next few days. I want you to see that all of their meals, beverages and gratuities are included."

"Mr. Lester," Claus said. "We certainly didn't expect all of this."

"Mr. Claus. It's a policy of the Casino Royal to see that our preferred customers are treated in the best of fashion." Lester turned his attention back to Webster. "You'll see to it?"

"Right away."

"I have to leave you now, but you're in good hands." Lester started to walk away, then hesitated for a moment. "By the way, there will be an immediate credit of ten-thousand dollars available in cash or chips at the Casino Cashier."

Jay-Jay gulped.

Webster had been busy filling out some forms. "Mr. Claus. If you'd just sign here, you'll be in your suite in no time at all."

"Thank you." Claus placed his signature at the bottom of the slip as a bellboy arrived, placing their gear on a dolly.

"If you'll follow me, sirs. Right this way."

When they reached the fifteenth floor, the elevator stopped. Following a short walk down a very long and beautiful hallway, they arrived at their destination.

The Bell Boy placed their key in the lock and opened the door.

Again, Jay-Jay was awe-struck, but this time Claus as well. They entered a living room area furnished much like the lobby downstairs -- several doors leading off in different directions.

The Bellboy placed their bags against a wall between two

doors to the right. "Will that be all, sirs?"

"Yes, thank you." Claus reached in his pocket for a bill as the Bellboy started to leave. "Here, son. Take this."

The Bellboy shied away. "Oh, no sir. I can't take that. Mr. Lester's orders."

Claus stepped forward and stuffed the twenty dollar bill in his upper jacket pocket.

The young man smiled and closed the door.

Claus turned to find Jay-Jay trying to figure out how to work the TV. "That's right. You haven't seen one of those in a good while." He crossed the room to join Jay-Jay. "Let me see if I can help."

Claus found a wire-attached remote control and switched on the power. The TV gained a perfect image of an afternoon soap opera.

"Ughhh. I can't take that."

Claus laughed loudly. "Change the channel. Here. This is how to do it."

Jay-Jay started flipping through the stations, as Claus sat in a high-back chair and started taking off his shoes. "Boy, these old tootsies are sure sore." He looked up to see that Jay-Jay had stopped on an xx-rated channel. "Aw, oh. Enough of that. . . . Find something more suited to your age."

Jay-Jay tried again and found a western movie.

Claus got up and moved to the phone. After a short pause, he said, "This is Mr. Claus in suite fifteen-forty-two. Would you please block-out the sex channels to our suite."

Jay-Jay frowned.

Claus hung up the receiver. "Do you want to shower first?"

"That's all right. You go ahead."

After Claus retrieved some toiletries from his bag, he started to head for the bathroom.

"Claus. What are we going to do with all that money?"

Claus stopped and sat back down in the chair. "What would you like to do with it?"

"I don't know. I really haven't thought about it. Everything's been happening so fast, I just don't know."

Claus started to rise.

"Maybe we could try to win some more."

Claus plopped back down in his seat. "Now, just a minute, son. I'm afraid I might have created a monster." He chuckled as he reached to rub his bare feet. "What happened back there wasn't skill, or even luck." He grunted and laughed. "I told you I was Santa Claus and you won't believe me."

"Yeah. I guess that makes me one of your elves."

Jay-Jay laughed as Claus almost went into hysterics.

Claus raised from his seat again. "Gambling is bad. Every winner eventually becomes a loser if they keep on going. You make sure you remember that. . . . Don't you think fifty-thousand dollars is enough?"

"I'm sorry. It was so much excitement and fun when we won. Watching all those sevens come up, and the bells and sirens going off, and all those people gathering around, I couldn't believe it."

"That's what gets most gamblers into trouble . . . the excitement." Claus headed for the bathroom again, but paused. "After I finish, I want you to get cleaned up and ready. We're going shopping for some new clothes."

CHAPTER VIII

"Jay-Jay, let's go down to the casino and take advantage of some of that credit we've got."

"Where are we going? What do you want to do?"

"Come on. You'll find out."

After arriving in the casino, Claus headed straight for the cashier. "I'm Mr. Claus. I understand that a credit account has been set up for me."

"Just a moment, sir," the cashier responded. After a brief moment of checking his records, he said, "Oh, yes, sir. I have it noted that you have a current credit balance of ten-thousand dollars."

"I'd like five-thousand of that in cash if you will."

"I'll have to see some ID."

"Sure thing." Claus reached inside his suit coat jacket and brandished the folder holding the voucher indicating their winnings.

"Yes, sir. That is quite enough." He opened his cash drawer and began to count out one-hundred dollar bills. "Will that be all, sir?" the cashier asked as he stuffed the money into an envelope and handed it to Clause. "Did anyone tell you that you look just like Santa Claus?"

"Yes, thank you. As a matter of fact, they have." Claus reached into his pocket and exposed another fifty-dollar bill and gave it to the cashier. "Merry Christmas."

The young cashier was dumbfounded.

Claus turned to Jay-Jay. "How about us going shopping?"

Jay-Jay nodded affirmatively with great expression.

As they walked out of the hotel into the bright sunlight, Las Vegas remained impressive during the day, but spectacular at night. The two strolled past towering hotels and casinos of all design and description.

"So, what do you think?"

"Geeze, this is too cool."

Claus smiled and patted the young lad on his shoulder.

As they neared a corner, Claus approached a policeman. "Sir, could you tell me if there's a Sears or Montgomery Wards store nearby?

The cop eyed him suspiciously. "Not really. There are several shopping malls on the near outskirts of town that have those larger department stores. May I suggest you hire a taxi to take you there."

"Thank you so much, officer." Claus again pulled a large bill from his pocket. "Here, sir. Add this for your next charitable cause. A very Merry Christmas to you and yours."

They started to walk away.

"Now, you hold on just a minute, there. Where'd you get this kind of money?" he asked, evidently unimpressed with the way they were dressed.

"Officer. I assure you it is mine to give."

"We'll just go down to the station and find out about that."

"Claus, why'd you have to go and do that?" Jay-Jay asked, appearing a bit more than concerned.

"To teach you another lesson in honesty and kindness."

The policeman motioned to a passing patrol car. It stopped and they all got in after being frisked.

Upon entering the station house, Claus and Jay-Jay were ushered to a long bench on the far side of the room.

"You just stay here until I can fill out some forms and see the Desk Sergeant," the arresting officer said.

As they sat down, Jay-Jay noticed a bulletin board near the bench. His picture was prominently displayed. "Oh, wow, Claus. Look at that," he said pointing to the wall. "We're in real trouble."

Claus smiled, and winked.

When Jay-Jay looked again, the picture was gone. He shook his head in disbelief.

"All right, you can come with me," the officer said, seeming to appear out of nowhere.

The two rose and followed him to the front of the station and stood before a counter and the Desk Sergeant.

"What do we have here?" the Sergeant asked, as he peered over his granny glasses.

The officer pulled the one-hundred dollar bill from his jacket and placed it on the counter. "This old gent gave me this."

The Sergeant raised his eyebrows and smiled at Claus. "And what would you be doin' with this kind'a money?"

"This kind officer gave us directions to a shopping mall and I was just trying to repay his kindness by offering the money to your Christmas Benefit Fund."

"Do you have any identification?"

"It's like I told the officer, I unfortunately left my wallet back at the hotel. But, if you'd like to call Mr. Lester at the Casino Royal Hotel, I'm sure he'd vouch for us. That's where we're staying, and I do have this." Claus retrieved the folder with the voucher of their winnings, handing it to the Desk Sergeant.

"Did you happen to look at this?" the Sergeant asked of the officer.

"No, sir, I didn't."

"Well, it appears that you have arrested somewhat of a celebrity. Mr. Claus, here, seems to have won fifty-thousand dollars at the Casino."

The officer gulped and reddened with embarrassment.

"And, who's the fine young lad you have with you, Mr. Claus?"

"This is my nephew, Jay-Jay. When I offered the money to the officer, I was trying to teach him a lesson in kindness and Christmas charity."

The Sergeant smiled broadly and confronted the officer. "I suggest this matter be forgotten, . . . that is if Mr. Claus doesn't wish to carry the matter further."

Claus returned his smile.

The Sergeant turned in his chair and called to the others in the room. "Hey, all. It appears that our finest new rookie has arrested Santa Claus."

The room erupted with laughter and cat-calls.

* * *

"Shuuuu. Be quite. Don't move. I'm Major Caulfield of the US Navy Seals." He had his hand clasped tightly over his subject's mouth. "How many prisoners are here?"

The startled captive spoke in a whisper. "Just three, as far as I know, sir."

"How are they dispersed?"

"Among three huts, sir."

A rat scurried across the floor. "Damn, I hate rats," the Major whispered. "Come on. Get up. We need your help."

* * *

Jay-Jay and Claus got off the elevator at the hotel's lobby looking like totally new people.

Claus sported a dark blue suit with a pastel shirt, and bow tie -- the latter being barely noticeable due to his long white beard.

Jay-Jay was clad in a charcoal gray blazer, light gray slacks, and shirt and tie -- both wearing new black shoes.

"Why don't we take a stroll around the grounds before we go to dinner. I checked earlier with the restaurant and they've reserved an open table for us no matter what time we get there."

"I'd like that. This town is unreal." Jay-Jay's smile reflected his continuing awe of his newfound wealth, surroundings, and experiences.

They stepped outside into a night sky of brightly lit neon.

"Quite a sight to see, isn't it?" Claus asked.

"You, bet it is."

"Come on, there's something I want you to see."

As they rounded the corner of their hotel building, across the street in the middle of a small park sat the largest Christmas tree one could imagine, ablaze with lights and decorations.

Jay-Jay gasped. "Wow. That's unreal."

"There's something else I want you to see."

They crossed the street and walked around the magnificent

tree -- a crowd gathered at the rear, all standing in front of a nativity scene. The figures were real people, and the animals all alive.

"This is what Christmas is really about," Claus said, as he patted Jay-Jay on his shoulder. "The Magi bore the first gifts to the Christ Child, not Santa Claus."

Jay-Jay nodded his head as he looked up at Claus.

"Ol' Santa didn't show up until almost four-hundred years later, and even then, he wasn't called by that name. Even today, Santa is known by different names all over the world."

They moved past the people and came upon a fenced area holding two reindeer.

"And, these are my favorites, Donner and Blitzen," Claus said, holding his arm outright as the deer approached and nuzzled his hand.

"Claus? Are you trying to tell me something?"

Claus chuckled. "That's all up to you?"

* * *

On entering the nightclub restaurant, the Maitre 'D immediately greeted Jay-Jay and Claus. "This way please," he said, picking up two large elaborate menus and leading them to a table with an excellent view of the stage. "Your waiter will be right with you. Have an enjoyable evening and dinner."

No sooner had he departed and the waiter arrived, accompanied by a busboy dressed as one of Santa's elves, who immediately poured ice water into two tall stem glasses.

"Would you care for something from the bar before dinner?" the waiter asked.

"As a matter of fact I will. I'd like a good glass of sherry," Claus said.

The waiter turned to Jay-Jay. "And, you sir?"

Claus interrupted. "Bring the young gentleman a Shirley Temple cocktail."

The waiter smiled. "Will that be all for now, sir?"

Claus smiled back. "Yes, thank you."

"I'll see that you get your bread and condiments tray right away."

As the waiter left, Jay-Jay shook his head. "I'm not used to all of this."

Claus chuckled. "It is a bit rooty-tooty, isn't it?"

Jay-Jay grinned. "Rooty-tooty? Where did you get that one from?"

"I keep forgetting you're not as old as I am."

Jay-Jay laughed.

The busboy arrived with a tray of bread, assorted crackers and cheeses, placing it on the table. "If you'd care for anymore butter or cheese, just let me know."

Claus smiled a thank you.

As the busboy left, Jay-Jay attacked the goodies.

"Looks like you're hungry."

"You bet," Jay-Jay said with a mouthful of food.

"Well, save some room for dinner."

The waiter returned with their drinks, serving Claus first, then turned to Jay-Jay. "Here you are, sir. I hope you enjoy it," he said, placing his non-alcoholic beverage before him, which was contained in a large fish-bowl shaped short stemmed glass.

"Hey. This is way cold," Jay-Jay said with a big smile.

Claus grinned and sipped his wine.

Jay-Jay picked up his glass and sipped from its lip; his nose spreading the orange-slice from the straw.

"Better get rid of the straw before you poke your eye out."

Lester arrived at their table unnoticed. "Good evening, gentlemen," he said. "I trust you're enjoying your stay."

"It's been great," Jay-Jay said.

"That's exactly what I like to hear." He turned to Claus. "Mr. Claus. I'll be in my office after nine in the morning if you'd like to finish our business."

"That would be perfect. I'll see you shortly thereafter."

"Excellent. . . . We have a terrific show tonight featuring Nancy Sinatra and Wayne Newton. Please enjoy your evening."

"We will," Jay-Jay said; his nose still in his drink.

Lester laughed and departed as their waiter returned. "Would you care for an appetizer before dinner?"

Claus looked at Jay-Jay. "No. I believe dinner will be more than enough. Would you give us just a moment?"

"Certainly."

Claus spread his menu and scanned it quickly as a young lady continued to motion to their waiter.

"Excuse me for just a moment. I'll be right back," the waiter said. He made a brief visit to the lady's table and quickly returned.

"We'll both have the stuffed lobster."

"Excellent choice," said the waiter, before gathering the menus and departing.

"This cocktail sure is good."

"So's the sherry. It's been quite a long spell since I've had any."

Jay-Jay began toying with his glass. "Claus?"

"Yes."

"What's your real name? You know all about me. You know my mom's name . . . my dad's name. You know where I live. . . . I don't know anything about you."

Claus sipped the last of his sherry. "Kris Kringle."

Jay-Jay smiled. "Oh, come on. I'm serious."

"So am I."

Their waiter arrived carrying a tray with two fresh drinks.

"I'm sorry. We didn't . . ."

The waiter interrupted his rebuttal. "You've been treated to the drinks by the young lady sitting two tables away."

Claus turned slightly and noticed an attractive woman giving him a huge smile and a wave of her hand. He blushed, and returned the wave.

"She said you look just like Santa, and to wish you a very Merry Christmas."

Claus cleared his throat. "I get that a lot. I thought for a moment I still had a little appeal in these old bones." He chuckled.

The waiter laughed. "If you'll forgive me, sir. You sure do resemble him a great deal."

The busboy arrived pushing a food cart to the side of their table. The waiter started serving their dinners as the busboy tied bibs around the two diners' necks.

Jay-Jay squirmed and appeared uncomfortable. "I don't like wearing this thing. I ain't no baby."

"Neither am I. Nor the other people in this room wearing them."

Jay-Jay gazed around the room, seeing a number of bibbed adults.

"Dip some of your lobster into the drawn butter cup," Claus suggested. "You'll soon find out why the bibs."

* * *

The hour was quite late by the time Jay-Jay and Claus retired to their room. By nine o'clock the following morning, Claus was fully dressed as Jay-Jay remained sound asleep.

Lester rose from his seat behind the desk as Claus entered the office. An associate sat on a couch reading a newspaper.

"Good morning, Mr. Claus. I trust you had a restful night."

"Good morning. . . . I certainly did. It's been a good while since I've slept in such a comfortable bed."

"Shall we get down to business? . . . Please. Have a seat."

Claus selected a chair across from the manager. A number of documents were spread across the desk.

Lester continued. "First things first. You do have the voucher from the café?"

Claus reached inside of his jacket and retrieved the leather folder, handing it to Lester.

The Cashier informed me you've only drawn five-thousand in cash against your account."

"That's true."

Lester squirmed a bit, and reached for his cup. "Forgive me. Would you care for some coffee?"

"No, thank you. I'd like to fill out the necessary papers if I may."

"Certainly," Lester said, handing Claus a form. "This first form is for our records as required by state law. I'll need your name, address, social security number, birth date and a statement as to how you wish to accept the money." Lester sipped from his cup. "We've already filled out the IRS and local forms, needing only your signature and the personal information after you've completed this document."

Claus began to write on the form as he spoke. "That sounds fine. However, the money is not for me. It's for my nephew Jay-

Jay. I'd like the balance deposited directly in the Riverdale Bank of Maryland in his mother's name. I've already prepared a notarized document stating the terms of the account. It will be for his further education."

"Oh. . . . You don't intend to do any more gambling?" Lester nervously asked.

"No. We'll be on our way. We have to get to the coast and I've promised to have him home by Christmas Eve." Claus paused to review the document. "We've really enjoyed your hospitality and I'll certainly put in a good word for you in some very important places."

Lester managed a weak smile.

"There. I think that does it," Claus said, handing the form back to Lester. "I've completed the information in Jay-Jay's mother's name. She's to be the trustee. I don't know her social security number and suggest you contact her at the phone number I've supplied to let her know what's going on. I'll speak with her tomorrow morning at the latest for confirmation. I've put my signature at the end of the form, plus other pertinent information. . . . Of course, I'd like copies of these documents before I leave."

"I just can't let this money go unless the tax forms are complete. You must understand that?"

Claus stood and moved to face Lester, placing his hands on the back of his chair. "Mr. Lester. I don't expect you to forward the funds right away. That's why I suggested you call Mrs. Anderson as early as possible to inform her of the situation. But, do me a very important favor. Don't mention my name. I want to surprise her myself. Then, you can mail either her or the bank the necessary documents for her to sign. There's no hurry. I'm the one at risk in this matter. I've already won the money. I shouldn't think you would complain about the extra interest you can gain over the next week or so. The paper work is a matter of procedure."

Claus moved to the desk and offered his hand. Lester hesitantly responded.

"Remember, now. When you speak with my sister, just inform her that Jay-Jay has won the money and that you'll be sending the forms . . . nothing more."

"Agreed." Lester turned to his associate. "Chuck. Make Mr. Claus copies as he requested."

"Follow me, sir."

Lester watched as the two left and closed the door. "Damn it," he said, picking up the phone and making the long-distance call.

The phone rang several times, before the answering machine responded. ". . . Please leave a message after the beep."

"Mrs. Anderson. This is Frank Lester calling. I'm the manager of the Casino Royal Hotel in Las Vegas, Nevada. I wanted to inform you . . ."

CHAPTER IX

Jay-Jay had already gotten up, read the note Claus left, and in the process of getting dressed when the door opened.

"Well. Don't we look chipper this morning," Claus said, as he peeked into Jay-Jay's bedroom.

Jay-Jay laughed. "Claus. You've been teaching me a whole lot. I gotta take time to fill you in on today's lingo. Cool, not Chipper." He laughed some more.

"Deal." Claus grinned. "But, for now, get a move on. We have to be on our way."

"So soon?" Jay-Jay asked. "Are we gonna hop a train dressed like we are?"

"No. Not at all. We're going to rent a car. We're traveling in style from here on. But, how about getting some breakfast first?"

"Fantastic."

* * *

Activity abounded at the base hospital in Germany -- reporters being restrained and restricted, as a frenzy of military officials scurried about.

"Who are they?" one reporter demanded.

"How did this happen?" another asked, trying to override his competition.

"Gentlemen, gentlemen," an appointed spokesman said to the

press. "We'll have answers to all of your questions at a press conference scheduled for later today. We have no comments, nor will divulge any names involved until the next of kin are notified. That's all."

* * *

A shiny-red convertible sped down the highway.

"Boy, Claus. This is sure better than riding a boxcar."

"See. You've learned another lesson."

Jay-Jay smiled and watched the passing scenery. "How long will it take us to get to San Diego?"

"It's a little over three-hundred miles from Vegas. What time did we finally leave the hotel? My pocket-watch is broken."

"I noticed the wall clock in the lobby showed near eleven-thirty."

"Sound's about right. I figure we'll get there about five or six this evening."

"Good."

"What kind of work does your mother do?"

"I don't know. . . . She's a secretary, I think."

"You never mention her unless I bring the subject up. You still upset with her?"

"No." Jay-Jay turned his back to Claus and snuggled into the seat. "Yes," he said, in reversal. "I just don't want her seeing some other man. My dad will always be my dad."

"I'm sure he will be. But, sit up, turn around and talk to me. There's something important I need to say."

Jay-Jay heeded Claus's command.

"You'll soon be eleven. Your birthday is only days away."

"How'd you know that? I never told you when my birthday was?"

"I saw it on your missing poster at the jail."

"Oh. . . . By the way, how'd you make it disappear like you did?"

Claus reached into his inside pocket and pulled out a folded piece of paper and handed it to Jay-Jay. "You mean this?"

Jay-Jay unfolded the sheet. "I didn't see you take it. It was there, and then it wasn't."

"There are more ways than one to skin a cat." Claus

70

chuckled. "It's unimportant."

Jay-Jay read the paper. Included in the text was a plea by his mother. Tears came to his eyes.

Claus reached over and patted him on his knee. "Life isn't always fair, son. As you grow older you'll understand much more. When you ran away from home, you really hurt your mother. Much, much more than she ever intended to hurt you."

Jay-Jay rubbed his eyes. "I know."

"Well, cheer up. I promised her you'd be home by Christmas Eve."

Jay-Jay's eyes opened wide. "You what? How'd you do that?"

"Remember when I went into the post office back in Kansas City? I sent her a postcard saying you were okay and would be home by then so she wouldn't worry as much."

Jay-Jay relaxed a bit.

"Why don't you lay back and take a little nap. You didn't get much sleep last night."

* * *

Sarah parked her car in the carport and sat for several moments in deep thought. She gazed around her and came to focus on Jay-Jay's bicycle sitting on the front porch. Tears came to her eyes.

"Enough of that," she finally said, getting out and slamming the car door shut. She proceeded through the gate and into her yard.

"Sarah," her next door neighbor called. "Got a second?"

Sarah stopped and turned. "Sure. What's wrong?"

"Oh, nothings wrong," Kim said. "I just need to borrow some vanilla extract if you have any. I'm baking some cookies. I've been waiting for you to get home from work."

"I'm sure I've got some. Come on in."

As they entered the living room, the phone was ringing. Sarah rushed to the kitchen to answer it. "Hello," she said, a bit out of wind.

"I'd like to offer you a special Christmas Prize from Jone's Pizza House," the voice on the other end of the line said.

Sarah interrupted. "I just walked in the door and don't have

71

time for this." She slammed the phone back in the cradle.

"Wow, you are upset," Kim said.

"I'm sorry. It's that every time the phone rings I pray it's Jay-Jay or at least some news about him. Would you do me a favor and turn the light switch on over there?"

"Sure. And, while I'm looking for the extract, why don't you check your messages. The way the red light's flashing on your answering machine it looks like you have quite a few."

"Where's my mind? I can't find it half of the time, anymore." Susan punched the button to rewind and play her messages. "The spices are in the third cabinet from the left."

The first message was a wrong number -- the second one from her sister Myra: "Hi, big Sis. I could'a called you at work but didn't want to bother you. Just wanted to let you know, since it's Saturday tomorrow, and neither of us has to work, and I'll be in your neighborhood, I'm gonna stop by and pester you for a while. Luv ya, bye."

The machine clicked through a couple of additional wrong numbers and another marketing call, before arriving at the message left by Lester: "Mrs. Anderson. This is Frank Lester calling. I'm the manager of the Casino Royal Hotel in Las Vegas, Nevada. I wanted to inform you that your son has been awarded a sum of fifty-thousand dollars that is to be deposited to your bank. You'll soon be receiving necessary forms in the mail. The benefactor wishes to go unnamed at this time, but stated he'll contact you tomorrow morning with an explanation. . . . Thank you."

"Oh, my God," Kim said as she plopped into a kitchen chair.

Sarah sat dumbfounded and speechless, her hands clasped over her mouth. Tears began to flow.

"Could it be true? Sarah, could it be true?"

"Oh, Kim. I don't know what's true and what isn't anymore. I just can't think straight. . . . What should I do?"

"Just calm down and let's talk about it. . . . Oh, darn. I've got cookies in the oven. Let me call Fred and have him take them out."

Kim made her quick call and returned to the table as Sarah was replaying the message.

"Fifty-thousand dollars? Who would ever give that to a child and someone they barely know?" Susan asked.

"I sure as heck don't know, but I'd sure like to meet him." Kim laughed, breaking the serious atmosphere.

Sarah smiled for the first time. She shook her head. "It's all so sudden, and unbelievable."

"Remember what the postcard said, that he was doing fine, and Donald said he must be in good hands?"

"Yes."

"I'm beginning to think that was an understatement," Kim said and laughed again.

"Do you think they were staying at the Casino Royal Hotel. Do you think I should call there? Oh, God, I want to so badly, but I don't know who to ask for."

"Ask for this Lester guy. He should know something," Kim suggested.

"How dumb can I really be?" Sarah got up and brought the phone back to the table. She dialed long-distance information and received the phone number, writing it on a pad.

"Hurry up, hurry up," Kim goaded with another devilish laugh.

Sarah smiled as she pushed the speaker phone and punched in the numbers.

"Good evening, Casino Royal Hotel," was the online reply.

"Hello. May I speak with Mr. Frank Lester, please?"

"I'm sorry, he's left for the day."

"So early?" Sarah asked, sounding disappointed.

"He's hosting a celebrity golf tournament sponsored by the Hotel, and actually hasn't been available all day. Mr. Lester is our senior manager."

"Oh, I see. I'm on the east coast and received a voice message from him. Is there anyone else I might speak with, like an assistant or someone?"

"Yes. Please hold on and I'll connect you."

Kim got up to hover over Sarah's shoulder, her ear near to the phone.

The phone rang a few short buzzes before being answered. "Hello. Tony Bartelli here."

"Mr. Bartelli. My name is Sarah Anderson. I received a message on my answering machine earlier today from Mr. Lester regarding my son and another man winning fifty-thousand dollars. Are you familiar with any of this?"

"Slightly so. Mr. Lester handled the transaction yesterday and I know little about that, but your son and his Uncle Claus generated a lot of excitement here. They had a great time last night being entertained in our nightclub by Nancy Sinatra and Wayne Newton. They sang 'Here Comes Santa Claus,' right at their table. I'll leave Lester a message that you called. You can reach him after eight tomorrow morning our time."

"Thank you very much, Mr. Bartelli. Could you transfer me back to the desk?"

"Certainly. Hold on just a moment."

Kim sat down.

Several buzzes sounded before the line was answered. "Front desk, may I help you?"

"Yes, please. Could you connect me with Mr. Claus's room? I don't have a first name or room number."

"Just a moment, please." The clerk put the phone on hold.

"Holy cow, Sarah. Who's this Uncle Claus?"

"I sure don't know. He doesn't have one."

The clerk returned to the phone. "I'm sorry, but Mr. Claus checked out this morning around eleven o'clock."

"Okay. Thank you."

Sarah ended the conversation by pushing the speaker button for the second time.

"This is all way too much," Kim said, leaning back in her chair and grasping her head.

"My head is in a whirl," Sarah said, getting up to go to the counter. "I need some coffee. Would you like some."

"I think I need a drink," Kim said, "but coffee's fine."

"What should I do? Should I call the police?"

"For what? They sure haven't done much to help so far. If this Uncle, . . . Mr. Claus, intended anything bad for Jay-Jay, he sure wouldn't have done what he's evidently done."

"Maybe you're right. But, why hasn't he just brought him back home?"

74

"I don't know, but it seems like there must be a reason for it if he's promised to have him back by Christmas. And, he said he'd call you tomorrow and explain."

"I just can't help it. I miss him so much. Ever since Joe died, I've felt so insecure. I didn't mean for it to happen, but now I realize how my reactions must have affected Jay-Jay."

"Now, don't go getting remorseful. This is a happy day. Maybe Mr. Claus is actually Santa Claus in disguise," Kim said, and laughed. "Be patient and wait until tomorrow morning. I'm sure he'll call. You have to promise to let me know right after he does."

CHAPTER X

It was just getting dark when Jay-Jay first saw the lights of San Diego. "Where are we going to stay?"

"While you were sleeping, I stopped to get gas and called a hotel for reservations. We're heading for it now."

"I sure am hungry."

Claus smiled. "The good life is beginning to spoil you, huh?"

Jay-Jay laughed. "Better than riding freight trains."

Claus smiled. "We'll stay there tonight and see some sights tomorrow and then go to the cemetery."

"I don't know which one it is."

"Just leave that up to me."

They soon arrived at the hotel and left their luggage inside the trunk of the car, except for two suitcases which a bellhop carried inside, as a valet parked their vehicle.

"Good evening, and Merry Christmas," Claus said as he arrived at the front desk.

"Thank you," the clerk said. "May I help you?"

"Yes, please. I have a reservation, . . . Mr. Claus."

"Just a moment please." The clerk referred to a log book. "Yes, Mr. Claus. You reserved one of our suites for the night."

"I did."

"Will that be cash or credit card?"

"I'd prefer cash if you don't mind."

"Fine. Just complete this form and I'll have you to your suite in no time at all.

"Thank you, again." Claus completed the registration requirements and a bellboy was summoned to the desk.

"Please show our guests to their room." He handed the bellboy the key.

No sooner had they gotten settled in their rooms, Claus said, "If you're as hungry as I am, I'm ready to go eat. They have a fine restaurant here."

"Last one there's a rotten egg," Jay-Jay said.

They both laughed and headed for the door.

As they entered the restaurant, a hostess greeted them. "Good evening. Table for two?"

"Yes, please."

She led them to a table next to a floor-to-ceiling window overlooking the water, placing two menus on the table. "Your waiter will be with you shortly."

Jay-Jay gasped as he gazed outside at the waves beating the surf and against the distant high cliffs under a moonlit sky. "Wow, Claus. Is that really the Pacific Ocean?"

"You can bet your bottom it is. But, I thought you were so hungry?"

"Oh, I am. . . . I am."

"Well, what would you like? You can order anything you want."

Jay-Jay opened his menu. "Geeze. I don't know. There are so many things. And I don't know most of them."

"Well, did you enjoy the lobster?"

"Oh, yeah. I meant, yes, sir. I really truly did."

"Then, may I suggest the Alaskan crab legs with broiled shrimp?

"If it's as good as that lobster, you sure can."

"Fine. I'm going to have the poached salmon. It's right here on the menu." He pointed them both out to Jay-Jay. "I have to go to the restroom and then make a phone call. You order if I don't get back in time. And, you can have another one of those cocktails if you'd like. Just tell the waiter. I'll be back as soon as I can."

"Okay."

Claus rose, left the restaurant, and headed for the phone booths. He picked up the receiver, touched the coin slot with his fingertip, and dialed his desired number.

The phone rang several times before it was answered. "Hello, and Merry Christmas."

"A very Merry, Merry Christmas to you, too. I hope I didn't awaken you."

"No. I was just finishing some dishes. . . . Who is this, anyway?"

"I'm Mr. Claus." There was a loud clunk on the other end of the phone. "Are you all right, Sarah. . . . Are you okay?"

She finally came back on the line. "Yes. . . . Sorry. I dropped the receiver."

Claus laughed. "I don't blame you for the shock."

"You weren't supposed to call until tomorrow morning, or that is what I was told."

"I know. But, I thought this might be a better time."

"Oh, it is. . . . It is," she said excitedly.

"Where are you? Where's Jay-Jay? How is he? . . ."

"Slow down a bit. I'll try to answer all your questions, but there's something I need to say first. When Jay-Jay ran away from home, he really wasn't running away from you. He was running away from himself and the things he couldn't handle or comprehend. He was very confused and lost in his own world of denial."

"Oh, I'm so sorry." Sarah burst into tears.

"Now, now. Calm down. Jay-Jay is fine, and almost through his problems. We met in Chicago, and . . ."

Sarah interrupted, through her tears, "Chicago? Oh, my God. He went that far on his own?"

"Well, yes and no. He did have the help of some new found friends along the way, but why don't we let him tell you about it when he gets home."

"Yes. I'm sorry."

"Stop being sorry. Nothing has been your fault. It's all been concocted in Jay-Jay's own mind. As I said, he's just confused. But a brilliant young lad, kind, generous without a fault, and has learned a great deal since he's been away."

"Where are you? Can I speak to Jay-Jay? Where is he?"

"Jay-Jay's in a very nice hotel restaurant ordering our dinner right now. I hope you will understand, but I really think it would have an adverse impact on the boy if he should talk to you right now. Please don't ask me why, but Jay-Jay is here on a mission of his own. We're in San Diego to go to his grandfather's grave. He'll be coming home right after that."

"Oh, my God." Her tears flowed again. She sniffled. "He didn't even know his grandfather."

"I know that. But, it seems his grandfather was the other closest male figure in his life next to his dad. It's very important to him for whatever reason."

"Please take good care of him and get him home right away. I miss him so much."

"I will. I promise I'll deliver him to your front door."

"What is your full name?"

"Santa Claus." He chuckled.

"I'm almost ready to believe that you are."

"I'm sorry, but I have to go now. I don't want to leave the lad alone too long. He doesn't know that I'm calling you."

"Give him a hug for me."

"I will. You have a good night's sleep. You're in for a big day tomorrow. Another Christmas surprise."

"Wha . . . What do you mean?"

"You'll see. Goodnight, Sarah." He ended the conversation.

* * *

All of the houses in the neighborhood evidenced decorations waiting to be relit after the evening dark. A number of neighbors were in their yards shoveling snow as a black car arrived in front of the Anderson home. Two Naval officers exited the rear of the vehicle and made their way to the front door.

Sarah and her sister, Myra, sat at the kitchen table having a bit of breakfast, discussing the recent events surrounding Jay-Jay and his new friend Claus.

"I just don't know what to make of it all," Sarah said. "I don't know why, but for some unexplainable reason I have all the faith in the world that Jay-Jay has been well taken care of."

"I don't know what to say either," Myra agreed.

The doorbell rang.

"I'll bet that's Donald delivering the mail. He can be a pest sometimes. I remember putting up with him before we moved outta this area," Myra said.

"You're probably right, but I don't mind. . . . He's a lonely soul, just like me." Sarah pushed her chair from the table, got up and moved to answer the door. She was stunned at seeing two uniformed Naval Officers, their caps held under their arms.

"Mrs. Anderson?"

"Yes, I'm Sarah Anderson."

"May we come in? We're here on official business."

Sarah continued to be confused and fumbled with her words. I . . . I . . . . Please forgive. This is a shock. Totally unexpected." She staggered slightly.

Myra stood in the doorway between the kitchen and the living room. "Are you okay, Sarah?"

Sarah turned to her. "Yes," she said, then confronted the officers again. "Please come in."

The two uniformed men entered and waited just inside the door as Sarah closed it behind them.

"Please have a seat. May I get you some coffee?"

"No thank you," the Commander said as the two officers sat side by side on the couch.

Myra remained in the doorway as Sarah took a seat in her chair across from them.

"This is my sister, Myra."

Both of the officers acknowledged her with a nod of their heads.

"Mrs. Anderson, the last time you were greeted like this it was with grave news. This time, it is much better," the Commander said, and nodded to his associate.

"This is Captain Killian, he was in your husband's squadron at the time he was shot down." He smiled. "Joe has been found alive and rescued from Pakistan."

Sarah gasped and burst into tears. Myra rushed to comfort her.

There was an extended pause in the conversation.

The Captain finally continued, "God knows we realize the impact of this wonderful news. There's no other way we could have informed you without it still being such a shock."

"Oh, God. Oh, my God. Please tell me it's true. Forgive me. I can't believe it. It's too good to be true."

Myra had Sarah in her arms. "There, there, sweetie."

"It is true, Mrs. Anderson. And we are as delighted about it as you are," the Commander said.

"Oh, God, thank you. Thank you . . . thank you . . . thank you."

Myra and Sarah started laughing through their tears.

"Joe will be contacting you shortly. I spoke with him last night and I can well understand your tears. I shed a few of my own. If all goes well, you will see him by Christmas," Captain Killian said.

"Oh, blessed Lord. I knew it. I knew it all along. I just couldn't let go."

The Commander stood. "If you'll excuse us now, we'll be leaving. I'm sure you and your sister have a lot to talk about. I almost feel like Santa Claus in bringing you this wonderful news. Merry Christmas from all of us at the Navy department and . . . gosh, from the whole damn wide world."

"God bless both of you. And, you are my Santa Claus. You're the complete spirit of Christmas for me. . . . God bless. . . . And, Captain Killian. You'll have to come to dinner after Joe gets home. Oh, and you're invited, too, Commander."

The two officers laughed. As they exited the front door, they shook hands and received hugs and a kiss on their cheeks from both of the two sisters.

CHAPTER XI

Walter Reed Military Hospital -- Washington, DC:

The nurse's station teemed with doctors retrieving charts and starting on their early morning runs. Doctor Presley selected two records and carried them down the hall, entering a huge ward. After making a broad survey, he headed toward a bed against a far wall.

"Kerryton. Is that right?

"Yeah." Kerryton groaned and rolled over to confront his visitor. "Oops, yes sir. That's me, sir."

"That's okay," the doctor said with a smile. "No need for formality here. In fact, you can call me 'Elvis,' if you like." He pointed to a plastic name badge saying 'Captain E. L. Presley, MD.'

"Oh, my God, Joe," Kerryton called to the next bed. Elvis ain't dead after all."

All three busted out laughing.

Doc Presley consulted the chart. "How have you been feeling?"

"Still a little punk. I've been vomiting a lot. Dry-heaves, too."

"You've only been here for four days. I see by the chart your food intake has been pretty well limited for a good while." He took a pen from his breast pocket. "The vomiting surely has

83

something to do with that. I'm going to put you back on a liquid diet until it straightens out."

"Damn, Doc. Don't do that. You have no idea how good it feels going down," Kerryton said.

The doctor laughed.

"If I have to go back on liquids, could you include a bottle of Jack?"

Doctor Presley shook his head, smiling, and moved to the next bed where Joe was sitting on its edge.

"Let's see who we have here. Captain Joseph Anderson, I presume."

"Yes, sir. That's me."

"From what I understand, Kerryton was with you in the prison camp."

"Yes, sir. He's hopeless, and probably one of the reasons I'm still alive."

"Oh?"

"No. It's not like that. He wasn't any outright hero. His nutty wit and endurance helped to keep me going."

The doctor scribbled notes on his chart.

"Doc. I've been feeling a lot better. When in the hell can I get this IV out of my arm? As much as I try, it just doesn't taste like filet-mignon."

Doctor Presley laughed again. "I see by your chart they really have had you on a soft diet. I'll see that it's changed by dinner time." He started to leave.

"Hey, Doc. When are they going to let us call home?"

"I'll see what I can do."

* * *

"Good morning, sleepy-head," Claus said, poking his nose into Jay-Jay's room.

Jay-Jay rolled over, rubbed his eyes, and yawned.

"Let's get some breakfast and then I want you to see something. Jump in the shower and meet me downstairs in the coffee-shop."

"Okay. I'll won't be long."

Claus shut the door, gathered some papers, and headed to the lobby. He went to the concierge to turn in the rental car, then proceeded to get some coffee, picking up a newspaper along the way. The headline read: 'MIAs Found and Rescued.'

Claus smiled broadly, folded the paper in half, and tapped it against his thigh before tossing it into a nearby trash receptacle.

"Oh, there you are," Claus called to Jay-Jay as he entered the door. "Over here."

"I'm starved," Jay-Jay said as he took a seat across from Claus in the booth.

"Hummmph," Santa said, the expression sounding like a grunt. "You're always hungry." His serious glare turned into a chuckle.

Jay-Jay grinned.

The waitress arrived. "Ready to order?"

"I'll have the pancakes, two eggs, bacon and sausage, and orange juice, please," Jay-Jay blurted without hesitation.

Claus matched the waitress's grin. "I'll have the same. But with some more coffee, please?"

"So, are we going to the cemetery today?"

"You bet we are. But, first there's somewhere I want to take you. But we've got to go by bus. I turned the car in to the rental company."

"Where?"

"That's for me to know, and you to guess."

* * *

The morning proved beautiful and warm enough to wear short sleeves. Jay-Jay had never seen Claus without wearing some type of coat before, and giggled at his walking shorts, large belly, bare arms and legs.

"So, you don't think I look snazzy, huh?

"Isn't that, Claus." He tried to compose himself. "I just can't picture Santa in shorts."

The two broke into laughter.

They reached the curb just as a bus arrived.

Jay-Jay sat in the window seat gazing out at all the passing scenery -- much of it glimpses of the ocean as the vehicle traveled down an adjacent highway. He hadn't realized they had actually been staying on the outskirts of the city.

"You know you have to be back by day after tomorrow. It'll

be Christmas Eve day."

"I know," Jay-Jay replied without turning around.

"Why don't you tell me more about your dad? . . . like anything you know about him. I know you loved him very much. Did he enlist, or did he graduate from the Academy?"

Jay-Jay turned from he window. "He went to the Academy."

"Wonderful. I'm sure you've been very proud of him."

"He's a hero . . . . My hero." Jay-Jay fought back tears. "He loved his dad a whole lot. That's why I want to go to his grave."

"I thought you didn't know your grandfather."

"I didn't say that. I said I'd never met or seen him. But, Dad used to talk about him all the time. He'd tell me stories about when he was a kid."

Claus smiled.

"He used to take Dad fishing all the time. My grandpa taught him how to throw a football. . . . You know, Dad was on the team with the Middies. They beat the Army both times he started as the first-string wide-receiver. He had a chance to go to the pros after his service time."

"You know. I think he might have made it."

Jay-Jay smiled broadly.

"Well, here we are," Claus said.

Jay-Jay had lost all sense of time and direction. He suddenly realized they were at the San Diego Naval Base.

"Want to see an aircraft carrier?"

"Oh, wow, yes." He leaped from his seat, urging Claus to get up and move.

"Calm down, now. . . . Calm down. It isn't going anywhere." Claus chuckled.

The two left the bus and got in line to be admitted to the base. A U.S. Naval Ensign dressed in Navy whites stood ready to lead the group on a tour of the yards.

As they turned the corner of a tall building, an enormous ship slowly came into full view.

Jay-Jay was stunned. "Oh, wow, Claus. I ain't never seen anything like that before. It's gigantamous."

"Gigantamous?" Claus chuckled and shook his head. "Come on. "They'll let us go aboard."

The majority of the crowd continued with the tour while a few stayed to inspect the ship.

"Now. You see that officer standing at the bottom of the boarding steps. When we get there, you snap to attention and give him a salute and ask, 'Permission to come aboard, sir.' Got it?"

Jay-Jay shook his head rapidly in an affirmative manner.

The two approached the officer.

Jay-Jay saluted. The officer smiled.

"Permission to come aboard, Sir."

"Permission granted." The officer stepped aside and saluted.

Claus winked.

As they gained the flight deck, Jay-Jay was in total awe. "Claus. There's a plane like my Dad flew." He took off running in its direction.

Claus ambled after him.

One of the maintenance crew attended a plane adjacent to the one Jay-Jay was inspecting. Claus approached him. "Sir, could I speak with you for a moment."

"Yes, Sir. What can I do for you, Sir?"

"My nephew's dad flew one of these in the war. He was shot down and I'd sure like Jay-Jay to get a better look inside."

"No problem, Sir. I'll take care of that." He smiled and turned to greet the lad. "How would you like to get up there and get a better look?"

"That would be great, Sir. Could I?"

"You bet." The crewman hoisted Jay-Jay onto the wing near the fuselage and followed him up to the cockpit area. "Now, would you like to sit in the pilot's seat?"

"Oh, wow, Sir. . . . Oh, geeze. . . . Could I, really?"

The crewman smiled and unlatched the canopy. "Climb on in."

Jay-Jay was in his glory as the crewman buckled him up and began to explain the various instruments covering the inside and the panel.

Claus stood below admiring both the plane and its current occupant.

The moment Jay-Jay's feet hit the ground, he snapped to

attention and saluted the crewman. "Thank you very much, Sir."

"A pilot isn't supposed to salute his crewmen, Captain." He smiled.

Jay-Jay blushed slightly as the crewman ruffled his hair and then shook his hand.

"Thanks. Thanks, again." Jay-Jay turned and rushed to meet Claus who had ventured further checking out other planes. "Wow, Claus. That was the greatest. The best thing I've ever done in my whole life."

Claus grinned. "Thought you might like it."

"Oh, I did. I did. . . . It was unreal."

"Well, I reckon we best be heading for the cemetery about now."

"Yes, Sir," he said with authority.

* * *

Jay-Jay and Claus got off the bus at the cemetery's front gate.

"You sure this is the right place?"

"It's what the lady said on the phone," Claus responded.

Just outside of the Cemetery a small stand offered flowers for sale. Jay-Jay selected a bright bouquet of mixed colors.

As they walked through the gateway, Jay-Jay paused. "Wow. This place is big. How are we ever going to find the grave?"

"Follow me. I'll show you." Claus headed for a large building not far away.

They entered and were immediately met by a clerk.

"May I help you?"

"We'd just like to refer to the Directory," Claus said.

"It's right over there," the young lady said, pointing to her left. "May I assist you with it?."

"No, thank you. That won't be necessary." Claus placed his arm around Jay-Jay's shoulder and led him to a stand holding a huge book and opened it. "This is the Directory. First, you find the name you're looking for. They're in alphabetical order, of course." He moved Jay-Jay to stand so as to read the volume.

Jay-Jay scanned the pages until; "Here he is. Right here."

"What does it say after his name?"

"Section Nine; Lot Twelve; Plots two & three."

"Think you can remember that?"

"Yeah. . . . Yes, sir."

"Come over here." Claus moved to a large map adorning one of the walls. "See if you can find the location on this map."

Jay-Jay studied it closely. Several moments later, he said, "There. There it is. Right there." He pointed.

Claus smiled.

Jay-Jay beamed with pride.

"Oh, Miss," Claus said to the clerk. "Do you have any smaller map copies of the grounds?"

"Yes, we do. You'll find them in a stand just as you leave the building."

"Thank you."

* * *

Jay-Jay and Claus stood before a single tombstone covering the head of both plots. The engraving noted two names: 'Marilyn Ann Anderson -- 1902-1964;' to the right: 'James Edward Anderson -- 1898-1976.'

"Are you okay?"

"Uuhhh. Yes, sir. . . . I guess." Jay-Jay paused. "I never got the chance to meet them. They died before I was born."

Claus patted Jay-Jay on his shoulder. "I know, son. I know."

Jay-Jay moved forward and placed the flowers beneath his grandmother's name, then knelt at the tombstone on his grandfather's side of the grave. He reached into his pocket and retrieved the naval wings his Dad had given him and began digging a hole at the base of the marker. He placed the wings at its bottom, covering the hole with the dirt, and wiped away tears with the tail of his shirt.

The two stood silently together for many moments before turning to leave.

CHAPTER XII

"Well, son, are you feeling better now?" Claus asked as they boarded the bus on their way back to the hotel.

"Yes, Sir."

"Ready to head back home?"

"Yes, Sir. You bet I am."

"Well, we still have the rest of today and all day tomorrow before we catch a flight to DC on Christmas Eve morning."

Jay-Jay displayed excitement. "We gonna fly . . . on a plane? . . . Really?"

"You bet. I made arrangements while we were in Las Vegas and here are the tickets." Claus brandished them for the lad to see.

"Too, cool."

Claus smiled and stuck them back in his pocket. "The flight leaves from Los Angeles Airport at nine a.m. day after tomorrow. Thought we might mosey on up that way and let you get a gander at Disney Land tomorrow."

"Holy, cow, Claus. You really mean it?"

"Yep. While you're here, might as well. But, thought we might do some Christmas shopping this afternoon and get a bite to eat downtown. I'm not going to ask if you're hungry, or not." He chuckled.

Sarah walked into the kitchen and placed her purse on the table, as the doorbell rang behind her.

The door opened. "Just me," she heard Kim call. She headed straight toward the back of the house. "Sorry to barge in. Know you just got home from work, but have you heard anything more?"

Sarah was abeam with joy. "Oh, yes . . . oh, yes. Joe called me last night. It was wonderful. He'll be here tomorrow, and Jay-Jay will be here the next day. Both of them home for Christmas. Isn't it fantastic . . . more than anyone could ever hope for?"

Kim took Sarah in her arms in a big embrace. "I'm so happy for you. You have no idea how happy."

Sarah smiled. "I love you, too. You've been my dearest friend."

"Well, I better go and let you get settled. I'll see you a little later, maybe."

"No. Please don't go, yet. Let's have a glass of wine together to celebrate."

Kim smiled and nodded her head affirmatively. "That's sounds perfect."

Sarah went to the refrigerator and retrieved a bottle of Asti-spumanti, and two chilled glasses from the freezer. She joined Kim at the table where she was already seated, popped the top of the bottle and poured the wine.

"There . . . there . . . there," Kim cautioned. You'll get me drunk if you're not careful."

Sarah laughed. "So what? Maybe it'll put you in a good mood for Fred tonight."

"I don't need alcohol to get Fred going."

They both broke into hysterics.

Finally, the laughter subsided and Kim offered the toast. "Here's to the most wonderful Christmas and to the most wonderful and blessed family on this earth."

"Thank you, Kim. To you and yours, too," Sarah countered.

Kim sat her glass on the table. "Well, aren't you going to get your messages?"

Sarah giggled. "I hadn't even thought of that. She went to the counter and returned to the table with the phone/answering machine. She depressed the rewind button and the messages began to play. Near the end, Claus's rich deep voice came loud and clear. "Sarah. Merry Christmas, this is Claus. We have a flight scheduled for DC, Christmas Eve morning, and Jay-Jay should be home in the early evening. We have a free day tomorrow so we're headed for Los Angeles this evening and are going to spend the day at Disney Land. My little Christmas present to Jay-Jay. And, by the way, I know how happy you were with your other Christmas surprise. I haven't told Jay-Jay his Dad will be home for Christmas." The message ended.

Both Sarah and Kim were in total shock.

Sarah sat shaking her head slowly from side to side. "How does he know about that? . . . He even knew before it ever happened."

Kim reached and took hold of Sarah's hand. "I wouldn't have believed it if I hadn't experienced it myself. I don't know what to say. . . . Could there really be a Santa Claus? I just don't know. What else could it be?"

Sarah placed her other hand on top of Kim's. "He's either Santa Claus, or the most wonderful man I've ever known."

* * *

As the two strolled through a large mall window-shopping, Claus paused to retrieve two one-hundred dollar bills from his wallet. "Here, son. Use this to do your Christmas shopping."

Jay-Jay smiled, took the money and stuffed it into his pocket.

"I'm going to get me one of those 'Cinna-Buns' and a cup of coffee over there. I'll wait for you until you're finished. And take your time. We're in no hurry."

"Yes, sir. I won't be too long. I've only got two gifts to buy."

Claus smiled as he watched Jay-Jay disappear among the throng of shoppers.

* * *

"May I help you?" the sales lady asked as Jay-Jay peered through a jewelry display case.

"Uh, Yes, mam. How much is that gold heart locket there

93

with the chain?"

"Let me see. You mean this one here?"

"No, mam. The one right next to it."

"Oh." She removed the locket from the case. "It happens to be on sale for forty-nine dollars. Are you sure you want to spend that much?" She smiled.

"That's fine, mam. Can I have it engraved?"

"You most certainly can, and it's included in the price. Will there be anything else?"

"Yes, mam. Do you have those things that hold those old type pocket watches?"

"Why, yes we do. We have the chain type, or the old leather fobs. Which would you like?"

"May I see them, please."

"Certainly. Just follow me around to the counter on the other side."

By the time Jay-Jay got there, the saleslady had several examples sitting on the display case.

"How much do the watches cost, too?"

"We have some that run from about ninety-dollars and on up. The gold chains run about the same. . . . May I ask how much you have to spend?"

"After I buy the locket, and with the sales tax, I'm not sure. I've got two-hundred dollars to spend."

"Okay, let's see what we can do. If I may suggest, this watch is very nice and it's on sale for one-hundred-and-twenty dollars. If you buy the leather fob to go with it, I'm sure you'll have enough to cover the purchases."

"Can the watch be engraved, too?"

"Absolutely." The saleslady reached for a pad and a pen. "You just write down what you wish to have engraved on each of them."

Jay-Jay immediately wrote: On the locket, please put, 'Forever, Dad and Jay-Jay.' On the watch, please put, 'Claus, Love Jay-Jay.'

* * *

"Come on now, you've got to get up. I know it's early but we have to be at the airport an hour ahead of time." Claus shook Jay-

Jay awake.

"Uhhh. Okay. I'll get up."

"Take a good shower, it'll make you feel better."

"I will."

Claus left Jay-Jay's room and closed the door and turned on the morning news. The TV flickered to life in time for coverage of Jay-Jay's dad's return home. The media engulfed the small residential area in Riverdale as Joseph and Sarah embraced for the first time in many years in their front yard.

"I'm all ready," Jay-Jay called, as he stepped into the living room area.

Claus turned-off the TV. "Good. The bellhop has taken our luggage already and it's downstairs waiting for us. We'll grab a cab to the airport."

* * *

Jay-Jay sat in the window seat marveling at the clouds hovering beneath them. The glowing sun was just beginning to set on the horizon, casting shades of many colors across their billowing surface.

"Well, son, we should be landing in DC in about a half hour. It won't be long now."

"Claus. Can you spend Christmas at our house, and with me?"

Claus chuckled. "You know I can't do that lad. It's the busiest night of the year for me. All those places to visit, all those toys to deliver."

"Yeah, right." Jay-Jay smiled.

"Seriously, thanks for the invite, but I really can't. I'll have to be on my way as soon as I drop you off at home."

Jay-Jay reached inside of his jacket pocket. "I got you a present." He handed it to Claus.

"That was really thoughtful of you, Jay-Jay. It means a lot to me."

"Will you open it now?"

"Now, lad? That's what Christmas mornings are for. I can't break the tradition."

"Okay."

"If you have to go to the restroom, you better do it now."

"I do have to go. I'll be right back."

Jay-Jay squeezed between Claus's legs and the seat and headed to the plane's restroom.

Claus removed his gift from his pocket and held it before him. He touched the top of the package with his index finger and it was as if the cover were never there. He read the inscription that was inscribed and touched it, again with the same finger, and the words quickly altered to read, "Captain Rudolph" -- Love, Jay-Jay and Claus.

He replaced the package into Jay-Jay's bag.

* * *

It had just begun to snow as the plane landed at Washington National Airport. The early evening air held a decided chill.

The cab pulled onto the Riverdale street where Jay-Jay lived. He began to exude some excitement, but also tinged with sadness. "Claus, I'll never see you again, will I?"

"I'll always be around if you ever really need me again."

"Are you sure?"

"You bet I am."

The taxi stopped in front of Jay-Jay's home. The two got out as the cabbie retrieved the luggage from the trunk. It was only Jay-Jay's things. Claus's bags had disappeared.

Claus bent to one knee and took Jay-Jay into his arms. "You've learned a lot, son, and you have no idea how much I've learned from you." He hugged him tightly and kissed him on the forehead, then rose to his feet, handing Jay-Jay a hard-bound novel he held in his hand. "This is what I was writing about. You can read it later." He tucked it under Jay-Jay's arm and turned to the cab driver. "Sir. Before you leave would you mind tapping your horn a couple of times to announce our arrival, and then you may go? I won't have need of your services anymore this good eve."

The cabbie did as requested and instead of the horn beeping, it played a chorus of 'Jingle Bells' that resounded throughout the neighborhood as he pulled away.

Jay-Jay carried his suitcase and small valise inside the yard and shut the front gate. As he turned to pick them up again, his mom and dad rushed from the house.

Jay-Jay stammered in shock. "Oh, Ga . . . Gosh. Da . . . Dad. Oh, Dad . . . I knew you were alive," he shouted as he ran toward them, dropping the book and luggage to the ground.

They met in a long and intense embrace.

Suddenly he pulled from their grasp. "Dad. Mom. This is Claus," Jay-Jay said. He turned and pointed to the street as the white bearded stranger turned to leave.

Joseph and Sarah looked up.

"Oh, my God! . . . Dad? . . . Is that you Dad? . . . It is you. . . . That's your grandfather Jay-Jay. He's my Dad."

Claus didn't turn around and kept walking down the street into the darkness -- his image dissolving into a mist.

Tears flowed from everyone.

"Oh, Joe. That really was your Dad." Sarah bent down and picked up the novel from the ground. They all looked at it together through glazed eyes.

The cover-jacket featured a picture of Claus and Jay-Jay. The title: 'The Littlest Hobo,' by James Edward Anderson.

THE END

ABOUT   THE AUTHOR

Shawn entered semi-retirement in 1999 and moved to North Santee, South Carolina following a lengthy and successful career in commercial graphics and the publishing industry.

He has had in excess of a thousand-plus non-fiction publications published over the years and countless working relationships with notables from politics, sports, and of the stage and screen.

In the mid-eighties, after the last of his brood left the proverbial nest, Shawn decided he would test is hand in writing fiction. The dreams of doing such having been around for a long while B the opportunity of finding the time previously unavailable.

His headlong immersion into fiction went even further than ever expected. Shawn took courses, workshops and visited seminars on writing for the screen. After joining a major international film forum located in Wisconsin, and associated with the University of Wisconsin, Madison, he went on to become the Executive Director until terminating his tenure in 2002.

* * *

FW: 497155
ISBN: 978-0-6151-3969-2

www.ingramcontent.com/pod-product-compliance
Lightning Source LLC
Chambersburg PA
CBHW030148200626
46812CB00015B/1750